INTRIGUING

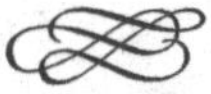

ALIE GARNETT

12-153-44 PUBLISHING

To all those who grew up in a small town and can't find their way back.

CHAPTER 1

OF ALL THE weddings happening in the world this weekend, Thomas Harstad had to walk into hers. Well, not hers exactly. After two marriages, Kit Kittson was completely over the entire getting married thing. Being a guest was as close as she was ever getting again.

It was his laugh that gave the four toddlers the advantage in the tickle fight. Before the laugh, she had them at her mercy, but after she heard it, she had all four climbing all over her. When she had said yes to watching the small children during the wedding rehearsal, it had been one little boy. Sometime between 3:00 p.m. and 5:30 p.m., three had turned into four plus her seven-year-old niece.

But at least her spot on the floor under the children made it so that Thomas Harstad wouldn't see her. How was she going to not let him see her here? Tomorrow she could skip the wedding, but today she was trapped. By four kids. None of which were hers.

Just letting the kids climb all over her, Kit wondered how sexy Thomas had made it to her hometown and into the church she had been raised in. Into her personal life.

Thomas Harstad was a part of her professional life—she was a history teacher at a catholic school two hours south of this church, this town. Far, far away from here. There, she was the hard-nosed new history teacher who expected more from a teenager than most of the other teachers. She was disliked by almost all students and even some of the other teachers, but she didn't care. She took her no-nonsense attitude from her personal life right into the classroom.

But Thomas, who was the school counselor, spent every contact with her trying to loosen her up. He was a constant flirt with anyone over the age of twenty-two, and he seemed to have laser-focused on her since her first day at the school. Her, Kit Kittson. She should have been flattered, but according to school gossip, he would never date a woman with kids. He wasn't raising anyone else's kids. So, she watched him from afar and let him flirt because it made her feel good.

Some days she just needed to feel good.

There was no way she would give in to his suggestions to grab supper or a movie or to go away for a long weekend, no matter how tempting it sounded. Because the minute he found out she had five kids, he would be gone, and the flirting would stop. Kit wanted the flirting to last as long as possible. Sadly, she enjoyed the flirting.

So, she spent her days appreciating his firm butt in the dress slacks he wore from afar—and those dark brown eyes if she was close enough. God, he was all around gourgeous. Not that she was looking … She was happily divorced and was going to stay that way forever. Two marriages were her quota, after all.

Five boys between the ages of twelve and six months was the reason she had no patience for the teenage drama around her, and it was the reason she was staying far away from Thomas. A whiny, lazy ex didn't help either because her ability to pick a man was not to be trusted. Another reason to stay away from the school flirt.

At work, she wasn't promoting the fact that she had kids, it was a catholic school with strict rules, and she was a divorced woman who had definitely gotten knocked up in high school. They frowned on those things there. And she in no way wanted to be pointed at as a warning of what not to do. So, she remained tight-lipped about it.

Most of the toddlers around her had gotten bored with the game they were playing and went back to playing with the toys their parents had bought or the toys the other parents had brought. Sitting up, she leaned against the wall so as not to be noticed, hoping the table in front of her was enough to block her from his view.

One hope was that he wouldn't recognize her, except she had just talked to him after school today about a student she had talked to him about earlier in the week. Kit had been leaning against her desk, waiting for the students to leave, which shouldn't have taken as long as it did for a Friday.

Or maybe she was antsy because she knew her older sister Mandy had sent her a text, and she had to wait for the kids to be gone before she could read it. Since it was about Kit staying at her apartment tonight, away from her kids, and she wanted to know the answer. Her divorced sister lived in downtown Landstad above the clinic that she was a nurse practitioner at. It sounded more exciting than it was; Landstad's downtown was two blocks long, but a kid-less night was excitement enough for Kit.

She laughed at her sister's thumbs-up text, which meant Kit was getting away from her kids! At least for one night. Mandy was spending the night across the street at her friend's place, which was a new ritual for her little friend group. A pre-wedding slumber party.

Mandy had moved back to their hometown less than a

year ago. Before that, she lived a few blocks from Kit, and it had been amazing having family so close, though she didn't begrudge her sister for moving back home. Mandy had needed a job not as stressful as a NICU nurse, and she had found it. Though she didn't seem to have improved much on her absent love life.

"Good news?" a voice came from the door. A sexy deep voice in the form of Thomas.

Today he was wearing his usual gray slacks and purple polo shirt, one of the school colors. His dark black hair was gorgeous and so touchable, but she had never actually done it, just spent time thinking about it. Way too much time.

"Best news all week. Unless you have better news for me." Shutting off her phone, she set it on the desk beside her, turning her attention to the man. Because he always got all her attention.

"I do. McKenna isn't expecting." He smiled at her as he walked into the classroom.

"That's good. Hopefully, she's learned her lesson this time." Kit knew the seventeen-year-old had not. This was not the first time she had stated she was pregnant. And based on the talk she had overheard from her and a friend, it wasn't the last. Some kids never learned.

"Probably not," Thomas said. He knew the girl even better than she did.

"Did you talk to her parents?"

"No, not unless it's positive," he stated, referring to the school rules.

"Stupid rule. I think they need to have a talk with her." She folded her arms because there would never be a talk until it was too late.

"As a teenager, would it have stopped you from having sex if your parents had talked to you about it?" His brown eyes were on her. Did he know?

"No, but I was stupid, too." She chuckled at her old self, hence the baby almost as soon as she graduated.

"Weren't we all?" He sat down on the top of the student desk right in front of her desk, his eyes running up her legs like a caress. "Big plans for the weekend?"

"Nothing much, just a small wedding of a family friend. You?" She slid further onto the desk and slowly crossed her legs. As she did, her skirt slid a little higher than it should have. Perfect. Five pregnancies, and she knew her legs still looked great. At least something did.

"Oh, mine is big. My best friend is getting married tomorrow. Love of his life." His eyes were on her legs as he said it.

Looking at him, she worried it was the same wedding, but no, it couldn't be. Her wedding was miles away in her hometown. The groom at her wedding was her pastor, and all she knew about Thomas's outside life was that he was a man whore. Seeing them as best friends almost made Kit laugh. "That sounds fun." Way more fun than a pastor and a neighbor kid getting married. But she wasn't looking for any more fun than a night without her kids.

"It's going to be. I've been waiting on this wedding since summer." Thomas stared, looking at her cleavage. She let him, wishing she had undone one more button on her lavender blouse; if she had known he was coming, she would have—once the students were gone. So far, she wasn't all in on the purple school color scheme, and replacing all of her orange attire from her hometown wasn't happening fast. Maybe because her own kids went to the public school, and their colors were red and white, so cheering on her kids in purple made no sense.

Straightening her back a little so that her breasts looked bigger, she was sure they were not going to be at the same wedding. Pastor Ruston and Hazel had only been planning this for two weeks. A bit of a rush, but Kit knew it would work out for them. From what her sister said, they were very much in love.

"So, I guess I can't ask you to go with me to the wedding, Kristiana." He looked up into her eyes again, calling her by her given name, the name she used at work. Because Kit Kittson didn't seem professional.

"I guess not, Thomas," she answered as if she was disappointed. With one hand, she tucked a strand of invisible blonde hair behind her ear to see if his eyes would follow.

"Maybe another time?" They did just as a text came in on her phone.

Picking it up, she read the message from her brother and, like the one from Mandy, it had a thumbs up. Maybe her siblings needed to get out of town a little more; they were really starting to act alike. But it said that her parents were up for watching her kids tonight so that she could get away. She hated to ask for babysitting help. She didn't want to rely too much on the older couple since she already spent every weekend with them.

"Got your hot date lined up?" He nodded at her phone but was looking at her mouth as she smiled at her siblings.

"Oh yeah, a hot little blond with blue eyes—you know the type. Stud muffin and I even have a bed for the night that isn't across the hall from my parents. Do you have a date for your big wedding?" It was the perfect description of the little man she was going to spend the evening with. Coincidently, his coloring was the exact same as her five. But then again, Hazel herself could be confused as a Nordskov girl. Her mom wouldn't even notice if she wasn't almost a decade younger than any of her kids.

Thomas laughed at her description and met her eyes. "Nope, hoping to pick up someone while there."

"Good luck. Maybe there'll be a lonely bridesmaid." She winked at him and slid off her desk slowly.

"With any luck." His dark eyes were on her.

"You probably don't even need luck, from what I hear." She walked around her desk, letting him see how tight her skirt was.

"What do you hear?" His eyes were following her as she went.

"Oh, I hear stuff, Harstad. I hear stuff." Sitting in her chair, she started to pile the scattered papers.

"Good stuff?" Getting up, he looked down at her working, most likely looking down her blouse.

"Very good stuff." She looked up into his brown eyes and smiled.

A noise in the hallway made him mumble something and look into her eyes for a moment. Then another noise came, and he straightened and hurried from her classroom. Kit watched him go and stopped her movements. His butt was heavenly today in the gray pants. When he was gone, she leaned back in her chair and sighed. *Hot!*

She should be ashamed of herself for what she had just done. Why had she even done that? Over the past almost three months, she knew he was interested in her, but just because she couldn't be interested in him didn't mean she *wasn't* interested in him. Because what she wouldn't give for a moment without those kids. Well, maybe an hour.

How could she have come on to him like that? Really? Her? She knew she had been blessed with her tall frame and a nice pair of boobs that didn't show that she had been pregnant a lot. Or even that she was still breastfeeding her youngest. Her legs were nice, and since she still ran every morning, she kept them in shape. Also, she had her mom's blue eyes and long blonde hair that all of her siblings shared.

Her clothes didn't hurt either; her baby sister Julia knew

how to shop and how to hand her clothes down. They shared the same body type and coloring, and on occasion, when they were able to go out just the two of them, they sometimes were mistaken for twins. But with only eighteen months between them, their mom probably would have liked them as twins better.

The temptation to just return his flirting for one moment was too much, and she had given in. Maybe a little too much, but what was the harm? He was going to a wedding tonight to pick up a babe, and she was spending her evening with a baby and her night without one. Finally.

But now she was here, and so was he. Why had she flirted so much with him? For months she had just let him flirt with her, and she loved the attention later. On the drive back to Landstad, she had tried to figure out how she was going to face him on Monday after that little scene. But since her older boys were in a constant state of fighting, she had to be a referee in the SUV and hadn't really had time to figure it out.

She had quickly dropped them off at her mom's with instructions on when the baby was needing to be fed. Also, with instructions for if her ex actually showed up for the two little ones. So far, he hadn't canceled by text, but he was more than willing to just be a no-show. Which would make this the fifth week in a row.

Then she had headed quickly back into town to her sister's place. Mandy was the oldest of the four Nordskov kids and had her own apartment over her clinic on Main Street. Math was two years younger and lived on the farm they were raised on. She herself was a few years younger than Math because her mom wanted a lot of kids and quickly. Not as quickly as Julia had come, which was why she was the baby. Kit came home almost every weekend, which meant only Julia wasn't in Landstad regularly. Her husband worked most weekends, and she worked all week, so coming here was not easy.

Mandy had been home when she showed up, and Kit changed from her wrinkled work clothes to the long, floral, flowy skirt that she loved and a matching pink blouse. She slipped on her favorite sandals she would have to put away after this weekend for the winter. It was always a depressing time of year.

Mandy was six years older than Kit and had the exact same coloring—light blonde hair and blue eyes—but Mandy was quite a bit shorter than her little sister and had always had a harder time keeping the weight off. But Kit loved her sister. Well, she loved them both. But it had been Mandy who was there for her when she had tiny babies and a husband who was in a band. It had been Mandy who had been there when she was widowed with those same babies. Mandy was special.

The sisters had walked to the church from there. It was only four blocks, and if they needed a ride back, everyone was going that way after the meal. That was the joys of a small town. In fact, they had only gone a block when their cousin Mia stopped with her red jeep and picked them up. The now short drive turned into a laugh-fest for the cousins. Mia worked and owned the café on Main Street where Mandy lived, and Mia lived in the next building over.

As they pulled up to the church, Kit had to laugh at this not-family wedding that suddenly had three Nordskov kids there when her brother Math and his girlfriend Tess showed up. Tess was very pregnant, and she was also a part of the book club. In the last year, a bunch of women from town started a book club. They met every two weeks and had a great time. The group didn't seem to have a lot in common when looking in from the outside, but they were a close group now. Today was Hazel's wedding, and they were coming in full force to celebrate.

She hugged her brother and, hopefully, future sister-in-law. Math and Tess had been together for a few months, and Tess was very obviously pregnant and had been for a while. So far, the woman hadn't said yes to Math's numerous marriage proposals. But Kit knew that Tess was having trouble letting go of her independence. Tess was the local bank's president.

Inside the church they all went to every Sunday, Kit was ushered away by the groom to the basement. There, his future son was playing with his three future cousins. John Henry seemed happy to have someone his age around to play with. Up until recently, Hazel kept him to herself. Kit had a son his age, and the two had never played together once, and she was sure they never would.

That was how she found herself sitting on the floor in the basement of the church, hiding from the guy she had basically thrown herself at just a few hours before. Glancing into the little room where she had confirmation class for two years, she saw the window was still there. Maybe she should leave. The kids would be fine. Right?

"Need a drink, Kit?" Sam Sullivan asked, snapping her out of her escape plotting. He was the history teacher in Landstad. He had not been her teacher, but she had talked to him often over the last few years about school stuff.

"Oh yeah," she said from the floor.

He handed her the plastic cup he was holding and smiled at her. "How is Catholic history?" He was referring to her job teaching at a Catholic school.

"Great." She took the glass and looked inside. Whiskey? "How is my job?"

He laughed at her question. "If you had gotten through school a little faster, it would have been your job."

It was the truth, and she knew it. Because when her late husband Jefferson had died after hitting a patch of ice after a gig late one winter night, she had pulled up her panties and used the insurance money to finally go to college. It had taken longer than she had wanted it to, but she had three little kids. Many of the classes she had taken were online, so she could work during the day. A four-year degree had taken her closer to eight, and during her senior year, she had managed to hook up with Brian Kittson and, whoops, she was knocked-up again.

What she shouldn't have done in that situation was marry him, but she did. Because that was what you did. And one had turned into two. But their marriage had imploded before she even knew number two was coming the year before. Brian had moved in with his new girlfriend—he has had three or so since then—and Kit had finally gotten her ducks in a row and moved to Grand Forks to actually get the degree she had been playing with for so long.

So, it was her fault she wasn't living in town and teaching in the school she longed to send her kids to. But instead, she was working at a school in the city and looking for something in a smaller town, closer to home. But there was nothing.

"I hear you have yourself a new lady." Gossip in this town was a sport, and knowing who was sleeping with who was high stakes.

"Yup, Natalie Beckett." He smiled as he said the name, but she didn't. She even knew it was coming, but still, it surprised her. Still made her mind race.

"Is she here?" Kit hadn't really wanted to see her. But it was a big possibility. More like a certainty if Sam was there.

"Of course, she's the bridesmaid." Sam pointed toward the kitchen.

"I didn't think they were getting along," she said quietly,

not looking in that direction. Hazel and Natalie didn't get along, hadn't for years. Though they were in book club together, Kit didn't think they were close. Not after … everything.

"They're both in book club, and it's helped them." Sam was looking at her, but movement made her turn to see Natalie, who was walking toward them.

"That's nice," she said, not knowing if it was an answer that made sense.

Natalie was years younger than Kit, so they never ran in the same circles, but what they did have in common was Natalie's accident. That was what it was called around here: Natalie's accident.

Natalie's boyfriend was the driver, and Natalie was in the front seat. Natalie's boyfriend had been brother to the passenger in the backseat right behind him. But right behind Natalie had been Kit's brother-in-law, Jamie. Only one person had lived through that accident, and it was Natalie.

At the time of the accident, Kit's husband Jefferson had already been gone for four years. Losing a second son had sent their parents to Florida, where their remaining son lived. Kit couldn't blame them; losing any of her sons to the back roads of Landstad would also send her a thousand miles away.

The happy look on Natalie's face said she didn't remember that Jamie was her relative. But he and Hanna May hadn't been dating for long, just a few months, when the accident happened. And Kit had been widowed for years by then. Not everyone in town knew how close she had been to her husband's baby brother. He was like another brother to her, and she had been devastated by his loss. She had even named her fifth son after him. James.

"How are you doing, Kit?" Natalie asked, as if there was

no past between them besides being from the same small town and this church.

"Good, and you?" They would see each other week after week at church, but she didn't think they had ever really talked. There had been no need.

"Mandy says that you teach in Grand Forks." Natalie made conversation because Kit knew she didn't remember.

She should be happy she didn't remember, except everyone forgot about Jamie. Everyone remembered the May kids, but nobody remembered Jamie. But she did. All the time.

"Kit's eyeing my job," Sam said with a laugh and got up to kiss his girlfriend. They were cute together. A nice-looking happy couple.

Natalie just laughed at her boyfriend and pulled him away with something about getting directions from Ruston. Watching them go, Kit wondered how wise it had been to come to Hazel May's wedding activities. Hazel had been Jamie's girlfriend's sister. Identical twin sister. It would be like watching his girlfriend marry another. Not that they were more than teens who were doing what teens did, but in the end, it was all they had.

She had known what they were going through. Jefferson Smith had been the love of her young life. They had been high school sweethearts since the eighth grade and had gotten engaged on her sixteenth birthday—secretly so as not to freak out her parents. They were married before the snow had melted their senior year and were parents that summer, and then again the next and, sadly, the next. What can you say? Young love. Would they have made it? Would that part have fizzled with time?

Nobody would ever know because just after Christmas, his car had hit a ditch in a snowstorm. He had been going too fast for the conditions. She had been raising their boys alone ever since. So, before she could drink legally, she had three babies with no daddy.

When she had gotten this job, she had been so grateful to actually have a job in teaching she hadn't even thought about her sorry personal life when she signed on to be a role model for religious kids. But now that she was there, she was keeping her head low and doing her job. Her personal life and past didn't affect that.

Weekends were spent with her parents, not that she wanted them to be. With shared custody of the two little ones, it was up to her to bring them to their father. And he was in the same town as her parents, who were a two-hour drive from Grand Forks. So, she stayed every weekend, whether he bothered to pick them up or not.

Hazel's John Henry brought her a book, and she gathered him onto her lap on the floor to read him the story. For a moment, she wished her own three-year-old was there also. But then no, this was her weekend. Once this little guy went home with his parents, she was going to her sister's place to drink and watch movies. Like the wild, single woman she was.

CHAPTER 2

SHAKING hands with Ruston's friend, Thomas couldn't stop staring at her. The lust he had felt this afternoon must still be affecting him. This random woman looked so much like Kristiana Kittson he couldn't stop staring at her. She was shorter and plumper, but he could have sworn they had the same eyes, mouth, and even face. As she spoke with Hazel, Ruston's bride, Thomas even thought they sounded the same.

Kristiana had definitely ruffled his feathers today. For months he had been flirting with her—not just flirting, but all-out flirting. Until today, she had never shown any interest, not even a flicker. But today she had turned it all on him in one ten-minute conversation. To the point that he had been willing to call Ruston and say he was busy, if only she had asked him to go with her to her wedding.

Since the first day he had seen her, he had wanted her. Tall, blonde, and drop-dead sexy, he couldn't keep his eyes off her. He had even hit on her that day, but she shot him down. That was her MO: she either shot him down with a joke or ignored his advances completely.

But for some reason, she had turned it all on, from letting

her modest skirt ride up high when she sat down to sitting so her breasts pointed right at him. It had been years since a woman had worked so hard to get his attention, especially one he was interested in. When she had sauntered around her desk, he had a perfect view of her perfect butt.

But what stuck in his memory more than any of it was when she was sitting at her desk, he could see down that purple blouse to the tops of her round breasts and the purple lace bra she wore. She knew he was looking, and it made it even hotter.

Now, hours later, just the memory of it made him shove his hands in his pockets so these people couldn't see how turned on he was. And for some reason, this woman reminded him of her. Not that he was even remotely attracted to the woman in front of him. But she looked so much like the woman he was attracted to, his mind was playing tricks on him.

"Where are you staying?" the blonde asked. He couldn't remember her name, but he knew that it wasn't Kristiana.

"With Ruston. So are his parents," Thomas answered, hoping he sounded normal.

Ruston's little house was going to be full, but with any luck, he would find another bed for the night. All he had to do was forget about a certain blonde history teacher in her purple bra.

"Hazel is staying up town tonight. The book club is having a little get together." The blonde was making conversation, but he didn't care at all about where the bride was going to be that night.

"I heard that, but I also heard that it was just going to be a drinking fest," Thomas said with a wink.

To his surprise, she had very little reaction but a wide smile. "You bet it is."

Thomas laughed as a man came up behind the woman.

He smiled the same smile as the blonde and Kristiana. Damn it, it was getting worse. Now it was men!

"Is Mandy flirting with you, Thomas?"

Yes, he thought, *Mandy*. "No, Mandy was just telling me about how she plans to get drunk tonight."

The man just laughed. "Mandy can't get too drunk because she has to make sure Tess stays away from booze. She can't do that drunk."

"I think your girlfriend has to control herself; I will be too drunk." Mandy laughed and wandered away.

Ruston leaned over to him and said, "Math's girlfriend is very pregnant. I think he doesn't want her to go to a book club sleepover tonight."

"No, I don't. But I can't stop her," Math said. He must have seen the woman he was thinking about because he hurried off as if he had something important to do.

Watching the blond man leave, he asked, "Are they related?"

"Math and Mandy? Yes, brother and sister," Ruston stated.

"They look alike," Thomas said. They both had the same bright blue eyes that had reminded him of purple lace.

"Yes, they do, they all do. If you see a Nordskov, they look like that. You'll get used to it; there will be a few more here tonight." Ruston's eyes watched his future bride talk to her friends.

"Any single ones?" Thomas asked, raising an eyebrow.

"None that you would be interested in." Ruston folded his arms with a frown.

"Is it a guy?"

"No, Kit Nordskov Isn't a man, but I don't think you would be interested in her. And stay away from her—she doesn't need your kind in her life," Ruston stated in warning, tearing his eyes from Hazel.

"Ouch. My kind? Thanks," Thomas replied in confusion.

"Sorry, but it's true." Ruston punched him in the shoulder as his parents entered the church.

Watching his friend walk away from him, he wondered what his friend really thought about him. So, this woman was off-limits. It kind of hurt that his best friend thought he should stay away from a certain woman. Or was it that he wasn't good enough for certain women?

Over the years, he had lived by two rules with women: nobody older than him and nobody with kids. He had been raised by a stepdad, and it had been no picnic. He didn't want to be that stepdad one day. He wanted his own kids, or in reality, he didn't want any kids. He spent all day with kids; he didn't need to go home to them also.

Thomas had heard a rumor whispered by almost everyone that there was booze in the basement if he tried hard enough to find it. And he was willing to do the work to have something to drink tonight. At the bottom of the stairs, he asked a tall black-haired woman about the booze, and she had made him laugh when she said it was in the microwave, but don't tell the preachers. Little did she know that the preachers would love to get into the alcohol. Ruston and his dad were always up for a drink.

Heading into the room, he watched her walk up to a man who was sitting, facing the wall, then he saw the woman who was sitting on the floor, talking to the tall man. Kristiana Kittson! This time, he was sure it was her. The clothes were different, but the woman was the same. Her hair was still loose and flowing down her shoulder as she talked with the dark-haired woman.

Kristiana was acting guarded. Was the man her boyfriend? But when the dark-haired woman pulled the guy away, he went willingly. The two passed through the kitchen, and Thomas asked, "Who were you talking to?"

He didn't know the couple any more than Kristiana, and

realized maybe he shouldn't have asked. Maybe they wouldn't want him to see anyone from this town either.

The guy looked back at her, and she was sitting with a little boy on her lap now. Reading. "Who? Kit?"

"Kit," the woman said and then laughed that they said it at the same time. "Kit Nordskov."

"Smith," the blond stated.

"Kit Smith. I forgot that." Her face fell, and all the laughter fell away. And her entire demeanor changed as she said quietly, "Smith."

"It's okay, Natalie." The blond put his arm around her and led her away.

Watching them leave, Thomas wondered what that was about. But for sure, the woman had many names. Like a fugitive. But looking across at her still reading to the little boy, he liked her as Kit. The name suited her. Since a Kit was a baby fox, and she was definitely a fox and a babe.

With a drink in hand, he wandered over to where she was reading on the floor. He knew she saw him coming but didn't look surprised. So, she had seen him first.

"Kristiana Kittson, or should I say, Kit." Thomas sat down where the blond had been sitting, his eyes taking her in, seeing the difference from what she had looked like earlier in the day. Usually, she wasn't so relaxed as she was holding the little boy.

"You can keep calling me Ms. Kittson." She closed the book, all the flirtiness from this afternoon gone. She had changed to a full-length flowered skirt and a pink button-up shirt that was so different from the clothes she wore to work that completely lacked color.

"And who is this?" he asked. The kid looked a lot like her, too much like her. He had never asked if she had kids. Perhaps he should have. Maybe there was even a husband somewhere. Here?

"Why, Thomas, do you not know the groom's son? Were you even invited to this wedding?" she asked, raising an eyebrow.

"Of course, I was invited. As were you, it seems. So, this is John Henry?" he asked, looking at the boy who had his head resting on her breast. What a lucky little boy.

"You should spend more time with your friends," she advised, her blue eyes were twinkling.

"They've only been engaged for a few weeks," he defended himself. But he knew he should have devoted more time to getting to know the woman his friend had fallen for.

"What happened to the couple you have been waiting on getting married since summer?" she asked.

"They only got engaged two weeks ago, but he's been smitten since summer." Thomas smiled.

"Smitten?" She gave him a half-smile.

"Is besotted a better word?" He couldn't stop smiling at her.

"No," she said firmly.

"Infatuated?"

"I will let you have that one." She chuckled a little bit.

"Thank you. Now you? Who are you?" He pointed at her.

"Me? I'm me." She put an innocent hand on her chest.

"In ten minutes, I have heard a dozen different names for you."

"A dozen?" Her perfect eyebrow went up in question.

"Well, mostly just Kit Smith and Kit Nord something." He knew he didn't remember the name, just that he should stay away from her. And he knew that Ruston had been talking about this woman, who turned out was the only woman here he was going to be interested in.

She just laughed at him. "Nordskov, Thomas Harstad. A good Norwegian should be able to get their tongue around that one."

"I was not raised in a traditional house where we learned how to say all the names." He didn't even know what nationality his last name was, but it seemed she did. It was just the name his stepfather had. A name he was saddled with at seven.

"Nordskov is my maiden name," she admitted.

"Smith?" he questioned

"First marriage."

"Kittson?"

"Big mistake of a second marriage."

Hazel called her name from the stairs.

"Kit? From Kittson then?" he quickly asked while standing up.

"Nope, I have always been called Kit. Just a part of my bad marriage, so I kind of stopped using it." She took his hand and let him pull her to standing.

"So, divorced twice then? Not exactly what the school likes to hear," he said quietly when she was on her feet and close to him.

"Then don't tell them. But it was only one divorce."

Hazel called her name again.

"How did you shake the first guy then?" he joked. Did that mean she was still married?

"I buried him not that far from here." She walked away, carrying John Henry with her as she went.

Her words stopped him from following. Maybe that was why he was supposed to stay away; she was a grieving widow. One that the entire town was protecting from the likes of him.

CHAPTER 3

DURING THE REHEARSAL DINNER, she was able to sit next to Mandy, who sat at the end of the table. Across from them was her brother Math and Tess. To her annoyance, on the other side of her was Thomas, and across from him was his sister. Really, their families were right next to each other. Couldn't she get any space?

So, there she was, right next to him, and the place settings were tight. Far too tight. She was having a hard time keeping up with the conversations around her. *Focus,* she thought to herself.

"So, what's happening tonight?" Math asked, mostly to Mandy and Tess.

Kit almost rolled her eyes. He knew what was happening tonight. Was he hoping to make Tess feel guilty so that she didn't go? Was he that much of a baby that he couldn't spend one night away from his girlfriend? Well, Kit knew he was because he was her brother.

"You're going home alone, and I'm sleeping with your girlfriend," Mandy stated with a straight face and pointed her fork at her brother.

"I might object to that, Mandy." Math sat up straighter in his chair.

"You have to let her, Math. You have no say over her life. No ring," Kit stated just as straight-faced. She could keep a joke going just as well as her siblings. "You should marry her."

Everyone who knew them knew that Math proposed to the woman all the time; it was Tess who was not ready. Kit was beginning to think Tess was just pushing her brother for being a jerk to her for the first five months they knew each other. Though her brother was besotted now, even Kit knew he had been a complete ass for too long. He deserved everything Tess threw at him.

"I live with her." Math put his arm around Tess's chair as if claiming her.

Out of the corner of Kit's eye, she saw Thomas's sister, Ashley, staring at the sibling set. The woman probably thought they were crazy. But what made it even more funny was that Tess Thorn was the bank's president, not some pushover. Even to Math, she definitely wore the pants in the relationship.

"A ring, Math." Kit held up her hand and pointed to her empty ring finger as she said it. Mandy next to her did the same—she was also single after her one failed marriage.

Tess was the first to break, even though she hadn't participated at all, just let it go on around her. It had been months since they got together, and she was now used to the siblings. Once she started, Mandy across the table lost it and was laughing into her napkin.

"I think you have given Ashley and Randy the wrong impression of our family," Mandy stated as if she hadn't started it.

Kit saw that not only were Ashley and her husband

Randy's eyes on them, but Thomas was also watching the siblings. Or mostly just Kit.

Tess looked down the table and said, "I'm sorry for them, but it's true. I'll have to share a bed tonight with a different Nordskov, which I regret. But the bachelorette party is a stayover event."

Thomas must have recovered. "So, are all you ladies staying overnight?"

"Only book club members, so Kit doesn't get to go," Math said, not adding that she was staying at Mandy's place across the street, but Math probably didn't care too much about that.

"That's because nobody invited me to book club." Kit looked at her sister, who only told her after the fact that it was a thing. Then suddenly, she felt Thomas's hand on the side of her leg.

"Sorry, didn't think you were interested. And I only found out about it hours before, because Mia wanted company. Besides, murder scares you," Mandy said, and Kit knew she was right. They read about serial killers every two weeks.

That was of no interest to her. "You're right." She bumped her sister's shoulder, trying to get away from the hand resting on her leg still. It didn't work.

"So, you three are siblings?" Thomas asked her family, as if you couldn't tell. There was no mistaking the fact.

"Yes," Math stated. "Mandy is oldest, then me, and Kit is the baby."

"Not the baby, that's Julia. She's not here," Kit stated corrected. Then she reached down and firmly pushed his hand away from her leg.

"And you two are in the book club, but why is Kit here?" Thomas asked. Why did she like the way he said her name? And why was his hand suddenly holding hers? When did that happen?

Pushing her chair out, she said, "Because I get to watch John Henry for the evening."

Walking away from the too cozy family groups, she walked toward Hazel, who was talking to her future mother-in-law and trying to keep the boy from leaving. Kit had been dealing with boys for so long, she knew what John Henry needed without even thinking about it. Better than she knew how to deal with grown men.

"Hazel, I'll take him." She took the little boy by the hand without looking directly at Hazel May. It was easier that way. Focus on the boy.

Walking up the stairs, she realized she should have said no to her brother on this favor. Even if Thomas hadn't come, the Hazel-Natalie thing was hard. Yes, she saw them in church almost every week, but there were always enough people for her never to have to talk to them. Tonight, there were not enough people, and they were everywhere she looked.

Walking into the sanctuary with the boy, she looked around at the familiar place. With the wedding, she had some decisions to make. Hazel would be the pastor's wife. Kit didn't dislike Hazel; as far as she knew, the younger woman was a nice person. Mandy had nothing but good things to say about her. But she was Hanna's identical twin, so every time Kit saw Hazel, she saw her sister. It had been six years, and she still saw her. And it hurt every time.

Some days she had to stop herself from hugging the sister of her young brother-in-law's first love. To ask her how she was, meaning her sister, not the living twin. Just once, she wanted to forget that they were gone forever.

Not many people knew that she and Hanna had become friends in the last months of her life, including her twin. At that time, Kit was a widow with three young boys and lived on the edge of town in a house barely big enough for the four of them. Her brother-in-law would come over and help her out when he could: mow her lawn, watch the boys, help with housework. He was a great kid. That last summer he had started to bring his new girlfriend, Hanna May. Kit knew the family from church and around town but couldn't tell the twins apart. They were younger than her by a half-dozen years and were always together.

Sitting down, she looked out the stained glass window, and just beyond it was where Hanna and her brother were buried, across the cemetery from Jamie, who was beside Jefferson. The funerals had all been right here, but she was glad she missed the funeral of the love of Jamie's young life. At the time, she had been too busy with his funeral to think about hers. Looking back, she should have attended it, but at that time, she couldn't. At that time, she didn't want to go to Jamie's, much less another's. It had been a double funeral for Hanna and her brother, Henry.

After Jamie's death, her in-laws moved to Florida. Not that she blamed them since both of their boys were dead. Knowing she should take the boys down to see them and actually going were two different things. What would they say after all these years? They blamed her for both their son's deaths. Jeff was her husband, and so it was her fault he was out with his band during that storm. And Jamie had been staying at her house when he was in the car accident, so not at their house.

Over the years, she had never told his parents Jamie was supposed to be at her house that night. Nor that she had let him go—he hadn't snuck out. Or that it hadn't been the first time she had let him go. She had sadly even known he was going to be drinking.

That night, she had been a twenty-four-year-old widow with three small kids, her husband had been gone for four years, and she missed their young love, so seeing Jamie and

Hanna in love made her long for the past and give them what she never had: freedom.

It had been her fault Jamie was out there, her fault they had the freedom to be out in the middle of the night. And she had known they were drinking. It was all her fault.

She always wondered if Natalie knew it was her fault. She must have. Jamie must have said something about why he was out that night. Hence why they were all out that night.

As she sat watching John Henry climb on the altar, her cousin Mia sat down beside her. Mia was a year younger than she was. But most importantly, she was in the book club. Mia usually had brightly colored hair, but today it was close to her natural color, brown.

"Nice hair," Kit said. She always hated the wild colors.

"Thanks. Bad dye job, and I can't fix it for a few weeks. But I'm leaning toward orange." Mia leaned back into the pew.

"But Halloween will be over then. Maybe you should do red for Christmas," Kit countered, loving Mia's disregard for what others thought of her. Kit had always been envious of Mia's ability to embrace who she was.

"I always do red." Mia wasn't one for same old.

"Green?" Kit smirked at her.

"Not again," Mia said with a shudder. "How's teaching?"

"Good. Students are OK. I do like it." She had been dreaming of being a teacher since the second grade, but life had gotten in the way for a while. Now she was doing it.

"But?" Mia knew her maybe too well.

"I would like to be here. Or at least have someone close again. Mandy is back here." Not that her sister didn't deserve to be back with the rest of the family, it just left her lonely.

"Maybe by the new year, I'll be there also." Mia's dream was always to get out of Landstad and live in Grand Forks or somewhere bigger, but Kit couldn't see her leaving. She was the town gossip, and everybody loved her. She even owned her own cafe downtown.

"I can rent you a room," Kit suggested.

"No way. Not with all those boys." Mia laughed, like always.

"Are you seeing anyone?" Kit asked.

"That is a tough question. Let me get back to you sometime," Mia hedged. "You?"

"Nope, I'm done with men and sex," Kit confirmed.

"Sex too?" Mia asked.

"That's where babies come from, Mia. And I don't need any more babies." Kit sighed.

"That is a downside, but not every sex act results in a baby." Mia blushed and looked around the church to see if anyone was close enough to listen.

"Far too many do. Just ask Math," Kit said of her brother, who accidentally got Tess pregnant when they barely knew each other. It had turned out great, but it had been bumpy for a while.

"I will bring it up when I see him." Mia chuckled, because they always teased each other. "I'm surprised you're here."

"Why?" Kit asked, curious.

"Jamie was dating Hanna, who looks like Hazel," Mia pointed out, always knowing what was going on. Even when Kit thought nobody did, Mia did.

"Yes, she does. I'm happy she's finally found someone. Don't think I won't be thinking about them tomorrow."

"Everybody will."

"What could have been."

"You're staying at Mandy's tonight? No kids?" Mia questioned.

"Not even the little one. Mom is taking them all," she said, feeling guilty about it again.

"How long has it been?" Mia asked with interest.

"With none? The night I was in labor with James. Sad, isn't it?" She shook her head and knew that it might be years before it happened again. Being a single mom means little downtime. Having five meant no downtime.

"Technically, he was there, so you weren't alone." Mia stated an obvious fact. Her mom had been there as well as nurses and doctors, there had been no actual alone time.

"Then it has been too long to remember." Kit sighed.

"Remember what?" Mandy sat down next to Mia.

"Being alone," Kit told her sister. Though she didn't go into too much detail, her sister was single and had no kids, so she was alone a lot. It was something that they talked about sometimes. But Kit knew it bothered her sister more than it should.

"Enjoy tonight, then. I don't know when you will be alone again." Mandy reached past Mia and patted her leg.

"I will. I think I'm going to stop at the bar and grab something to go." She laughed at what she had just said. "Landstad doesn't have fast food, but we have fast booze."

"That we do. And a short walk to my place," Mandy agreed.

Math sat down by Mandy, slipping his arm around his sister, and said, "Family reunion?"

"You bet, any more in the room?" Mia asked, looking around.

"Okay, everyone, we are going to start the rehearsal. So, everyone in the wedding come forward, and everyone else to the back," Thomas announced as he walked past her, heading for the front of the church. How had he gotten so close, and she didn't notice?

Grabbing the little boy and heading to the back of the church, she sat down again to wait and gave John Henry a small car she had in her pocket. Handing it to the boy, someone sat down beside her. It was Thomas's sister. She had been surprised when Ruston's twin brother's wife was Thomas's sister.

"So, you are in charge of John Henry?" Ashley asked. She was carrying a baby, who was a few months younger than James, but hers was a girl, based on all the pink.

"Yes, he's my date." Kit smiled at the woman, who looked only a little like Thomas with her red hair and blue eyes.

"I love that Ruston is going to have a kid. He's always been so good with them."

"He found a good wife also. Hazel is great." She hoped she sold it.

"Do you know her well?" Ashley asked, bouncing the baby in her arms.

"Not really. We're six years apart, and this being a small town, I know of her more than I know her. But we went to the same church and school. My sister Mandy knows her well," she explained, hoping it was enough. Because she wasn't going to tell this woman why they weren't close.

"Is she the tall one?" Ashley pointed to Natalie.

"No, that's Natalie. My sister is Mandy. Looks like me but shorter and older." She pointed across the pews to her sister sitting next to Tess.

"OK. It's a lot of people," Ashley stated with a smile. "Do you know Thomas?"

Kit's eyes looked to the front, where he was talking with the bride and groom. But then he looked up at her, then looked away quickly.

"Yes, I teach at the same school," she admitted, even if she didn't want to. She didn't even know why she didn't want to tell the woman they worked together.

"Small world." Ashley smirked and shifted the baby in her arms.

"It is," Kit agreed. "What's the baby's name?"

"Brielle." Ashley lifted the baby so that Kit could see her face. "Do you have any of your own?"

Kit analyzed Ashley. She could easily lie to her, and she would probably never know. They would most likely never run into each other again. And she was Thomas's sister.

"Five boys," she admitted.

"Wow, we have the one boy, and I was so happy that this one is a girl. Five?" Ashley said what most people said. Kit had not set out for five, five just happened.

"They are crazy," Kit admitted. It was what everyone wanted to know next.

"How old?" Kit could see she was looking at her brother. She was going to tell him ASAP.

"Twelve, eleven, ten, three, and six months," Kit said.

"Where is your husband tonight?"

"Probably with his girlfriend. We're divorced. My mom has the kids for the evening." When asked, she rarely talked about Jeff. It was easier to say divorced. No condolence that always accompanied the widow statement, no sympathy or questions. When you say divorced, nobody asks a thing.

Ashley just looked at her and then looked at Thomas in the front. Then she smiled at Kit and laughed. A very devious sisterly laugh.

"What?" Kit was getting uncomfortable.

"Thomas hasn't been able to keep his eyes off you all night." Ashley was still chuckling as she looked at her brother in front of them, explaining the ceremony to those who were going to be in it.

"I don't think so," Kit denied, but she knew she hadn't been able to keep her eyes off him.

"Yup, and you're going to make him break all his stupid rules."

"No. Once he knows, he won't be interested anymore."

There, she said it out loud. It was real, what she had always known.

"I'm not going to tell him. He needs this," Ashley said.

"You don't have his back?" she questioned. Don't all siblings have each other's backs?

"Nope. But from how your siblings are, they would do the same thing for you." Ashley looked over at Mandy and Math, who were arguing quietly a few pews in front of them.

"Probably," Kit admitted, looking over at her own siblings. That was exactly what they would do.

CHAPTER 4

ASHLEY WAS SITTING WITH HER. What was his sister telling her? What could they possibly be talking about? His awkward teen years? His inability to commit? His hatred of green beans? His sister knew too much.

Turning back to the groom, who was happily staring into his bride's eyes, he almost forgot about his sister sitting with Kit Kittson. Really! Foxy Kit. Kit with the sexy laugh. Kit with the purple lace bra. Kit at Ruston's wedding.

Walking the couple through what was going to happen at the wedding the next day, he kept catching glimpses of foxy Kit. After his sister and Randy left for the long drive back home, she had talked to a white-haired woman and her boyfriend for a while. Then her siblings migrated back to sit with her. They seemed to always be near, a bit protective. Not just against men who want to approach her, but from everyone.

Or maybe he had been reading it all wrong. Maybe the siblings just got along well and liked spending time together. Some families were like that. Ruston's family always got along. His own? Not as much. In fact, he had always liked

Ruston's family better than his and spent more time there than at home. One of his happiest days was when Ashley married Randy and joined the family. He always felt that he was now a member because of it.

By the time everyone knew what they had to do the next day, Ruston's family and most of the men of the book club members had left. Math was still there, and so was Sam, the blond guy Kit had been talking to. He was the boyfriend of the bridesmaid. Ruston's brother Randy was the groomsman, and to Thomas's surprise, they wouldn't be standing with the couple during the ceremony. The couple would stand alone.

Most of the wedding had been planned by the bridesmaid, Natalie. All except that detail. Though once she heard about it, she got teary-eyed and gave the bride a hug.

Thomas was sure the small group of men would all be up for a good time. It was time to see Ruston let loose one last time. Or to be more precise, the only time. Though it was going to be a hard sell. Thomas was sure that with enough guys, he could make it happen.

"So, are the bachelors going out?" Thomas asked Ruston and Sam, who were standing near him, talking about someone Thomas didn't know.

"Nope. I have John Henry tonight." Ruston pointed at Hazel, who was now holding the boy, talking to her friends on the other side of the room.

"That's why you have parents, Rusty. Sam, are you in?"

"I don't know. Landstad isn't exactly the best place for a bachelor party," Sam stated.

"So, we are all going home at 8:00 p.m.? Can we watch some movies on the couch too? Pop some popcorn? Gossip?" Thomas said sarcastically. There had to be more to do in this town.

"You can go out and drink if you want, Thomas, but I

want to be completely sober when I get married," Ruston stated as Sam left to say goodbye to his girlfriend.

Then Ruston wandered toward the women gathering up their stuff to leave. Sadly, Kit was leaving with them. As a small herd, he watched them file out the door, unable to talk to her in private.

As they left, he kind of wanted to join the book club party. It was going to be way better than anything else happening in this town tonight. Sam and Math followed behind the women, and he knew they would gladly attend also.

With them gone, it left Ruston and Thomas alone. Ruston had to make sure the church was in order for the morning, and Thomas had nothing else to do, so he stayed. After all, Kit was gone, and he had no way to even know where she went. The town was small but not that small.

"So, how excited are you to marry this woman?" Thomas helped Ruston pick up wayward cups and plates. For a small crowd, they had made quite the mess.

"I can't even put it into words," Ruston admitted with a grin that so far, Thomas hadn't seen on the guy's face. "It's like it's my sixteenth birthday, and I know Mom and Dad bought me a new car. All I have to do is wait until tomorrow to get it, but I already know how great it is going to be."

Thomas laughed at his friend's analogy; both would have killed for just a car when they were in high school, but neither had one. Though Thomas's parents could have afforded it, his stepdad had insisted he earn the money himself. But then he immediately stated that no kid of his would do any of the jobs that sixteen-year-olds were qualified for. So, he hadn't gotten a car until college, and then just barely.

"What about the kid?" Thomas asked about his friend's soon-to-be stepson. Ruston's parents had taken him to

Ruston's house already. His parents were all about the grand-kids, always had been.

"What about him?" Ruston asked in question.

"You can't tell me you're excited that she had a kid. That you have to raise someone else's kid."

"I guess I always knew about him, so it was no big deal. They were two the entire time. You have to get over the fear of women and kids." Ruston tossed a paper plate at him.

"You go ahead and marry this woman with a kid, leave me to me." He tossed it back.

"I will, and I hope one day you fall for a woman with like half a dozen of them." Ruston laughed as he threw the garbage in his hand into the trash can.

"And a curse on your household as well," Thomas shot back at him, doing the same.

"You can't just vague curse me." Ruston shut off the lights in the basement.

"May your future bride produce for you twins at every birth." He pointed at Ruston as they climbed the stairs.

"Curses can't be something that might happen, Thomas." Ruston and Hazel were both the product of multiple births, so maybe twins weren't too far out of the question. But it was something that made Thomas shudder to even think about, so he wasn't taking it back.

"I don't care. Every birth, at least two, maybe more." He held up two fingers at his friend.

Ruston laughed as he opened the door for Thomas to leave the building. "Your curse is my wish, my friend."

Watching Ruston lock the door, he asked, "Are you really not going out with me tonight? I would like to find a date for your wedding."

"Nope, I have to get ready for my wedding. You probably should too. I would appreciate you being sober tomorrow, also." Ruston's words were more of a warning than advice.

"I'm ready. I think I'll check out the bar down there for a bit, then I will come home. Mostly sober to sleep alone on your couch. I bet it's lumpy too."

They walked to Ruston's house as he looked down the street for the sign called The Landing.

"It'll be dead, but enjoy yourself." Ruston turned to walk up his walkway, and Thomas headed toward the only place in town that sold liquor.

Of course, Ruston had been right. The bar was dead. There were six people there, and that included the bartender. Of the five, four were men, and one was a waitress—not a good-looking one, either. Glancing at the clock on the wall, he knew he would be on that couch in an hour.

Taking a seat at the bar, he ordered a beer and listened to the country music coming from the speakers. Not his favorite genre, but the depressing music was exactly what this place needed. All it was missing was some drunk guy crying in the corner, but so far tonight, all corners were empty.

Since there was nothing to keep his mind off Kit Kittson, it drifted right to her. Since the first day, he had thought she was gorgeous, but today, he had actually seen more of her personality then she had ever let slip at school. The strict, humorless, by-the-book history teacher she presented every day was a facade. She was quick with a comeback and teased those she knew mercilessly. And the memory of her laugh made him hard. He was like a teenager around her today, unable to control his own body.

Tomorrow, he decided, he was going to see if he could find the flirty Kit, the one from school today. She was in there somewhere, and he had the entire reception and dance to find her. She had to be at the wedding—she was at the rehearsal dinner, after all.

Would she wear the long flowy skirt tomorrow or would

she wear a tighter one, the shorter one that shows off those legs? Maybe she would wear something completely different, so he would have another outfit to peel off her in his fantasies.

Deciding he would finish his beer and head out, he almost choked on the next sip when Kit walked out of his fantasies and into the bar. She was still wearing the same outfit she had been in at the dinner, and she seemed familiar with not just the bar but most of the men in it since she waved or said hello to more than one as she passed by.

She didn't see him; he could tell.

First, she walked right up to the bar and asked the bartender for her drink, then the guy on her other side caught her attention. Thomas watched as the two hugged, and she sat down next to him at the bar. The two chatted and laughed a little too much for Thomas's liking.

Leaving his half-empty beer, he headed over to talk to the happy pair. Her smile faded as he walked up to them, but the man's didn't.

"Kit, fancy meeting you here," Thomas said lamely, leaning against the bar right next to the stool she sat down on.

It was a jerk thing to do. He had no claim on the woman, but he wanted the man on the other side of her to think he did. That she was his.

"It's the only bar in town, Thomas," she pointed out.

"The best bar in town," the man she was talking to said and held his drink up in the air for a cheer.

"Sorry, Thomas, we are in the middle of a class reunion here." Then she laughed. "Sorry, too much whiskey at the rehearsal dinner."

"Mia." He shook his head with a smile.

"Rafferty, are you still hung up on Mia?" She bumped him on the shoulder with her fist.

"No, I'm not." Rafferty laughed at her and looked at his phone. "Anderson is at my place. Ruth kicked him out for the party, so I get a sappy-in-love roommate for the night."

"I talked to them tonight," Kit told him, ignoring Thomas completely.

"Were they sappy?" Rafferty asked in disgust.

"Didn't seem like it. I like that she really seems happy, though," Kit said, not acknowledging Thomas at all.

That man shrugged. "Yeah, he does really make her happy. He's my boss now."

"That's what I heard." Kit grinned, not saying anymore.

The man quirked an eyebrow at her.

She shrugged. "Mia."

The man said goodbye and left to spend the evening with his homeless friend. It seemed like the entire town was affected by the ladies gathering tonight. Thomas watched Kit swivel her stool away from him and watch the man go.

"So, was that the entire class?" he asked her.

She was still facing away from him, watching her friend leave. "Ha ha. We had twenty-four graduates, for your information." She turned back to him with those gorgeous blue eyes.

"Such lofty numbers." He put his hand on her back.

"We were a smaller class." She didn't move away from his touch, unlike at the dinner.

"Why is the bar dead on a Friday night?" He ran his hand slowly down her back.

"Because if you really want to party, you leave town on the weekends. It's busier on weeknights when people don't want to travel for booze." She looked around at the empty bar. This time she had turned her stool toward him, not away.

"But you came in?" he pointed out.

She stayed facing him but looked around the room. "That I did," she whispered and turned her eyes back to his.

"Sorry that took so long, Kit. I had a phone call," the bartender said from far away.

But it was enough that she jerked away from his gaze and turned to the man. "Thanks, Paul." She handed him her credit card. Her eyes stayed away from Thomas, but he just looked at the side of her head. That blonde hair was as natural as she was. Even without seeing her siblings, who both were as blond as her, he knew it was real.

"Have a nice night," the bartender said with a quick smile before turning to another customer.

"Thanks." She turned her stool away from Thomas, slipped off, and headed for the door.

With nothing better to do, he followed her, close enough that he was able to open the door for her. Once outside, she turned and headed down the sidewalk, trying to get away from him.

"What do you have?" he asked about the brown bag she was carrying.

"Nothing." She didn't stop.

Thomas grabbed it out of her hand, stopping her instantly.

Turning, she glared at him, "That is mine."

Looking in the bag, he whistled. "Wine coolers, Kit? Classy."

"Shut up." He handed the bag back to her. She held it to her chest.

"Big plans for your evening?" He stepped closer, and she stepped back.

"Yes, alone." Her back hit the wall behind her, and he took another step closer.

"Want company?" He put a finger under her chin and tilted her head up so that he could look into her blue eyes.

"That would defeat the meaning of being *alone*." She licked her bottom lip.

"Exactly." His lips touched the wet of the lip she had just licked.

Naturally, she tasted better than he had ever dreamed she would: a little whiskey, a little strawberry from the dessert, and a whole lot of Kit. His lips pressed firmer to hers, and to his surprise, she responded by returning the kiss with enthusiasm. He pulled her tighter to him as he reached between them and pulled out the bag of alcohol. Dropping it on the ground at his feet, he didn't even check to see if he broke any of the bottles. Her arms empty, they slid up his chest and went around his neck.

Her body against his was everything he had hoped it would be. Perfect. Running his hand up her back, keeping her close as he pulled his mouth from hers, he gently bit her ear as he whispered, "Please tell me you have a place here."

Her answer was a moaned whisper, "We shouldn't do this."

"Yes, we should." His lips went down her skin to her neck.

"We work together. This shouldn't be happening." Her head tilted to give him better access.

"Kit, stop overthinking." He bit her lightly, and his hands slid under her shirt and up her smooth warm back, needing to touch her.

"Thomas, start thinking a little," she said on a sigh.

"I'm thinking about ripping this shirt off you in the middle of downtown." His thumbs ran across the underside of her bra.

"Right here." Her voice was husky.

"Yes, right here." His lips moved down to the V of her shirt.

"No, I'm staying right here, upstairs." She pushed him away and took his hand.

They both ignored the bag on the ground as she pulled him back toward the bar and past two businesses before opening a glass door and pulling him inside, taking them into a stairway with a small landing.

Pushing her against the wall again, he slipped his hands inside her shirt, this time cupping her breast. Feeling their warm perfection under his fingers. "You walked past this place."

"You were following me." Her voice was husky again.

His mouth was on hers again, not caring anymore now that he had her here, private if it wasn't for the glass door they had just come through. Unable to get enough of her, to get close enough to her, he growled when she grabbed his shirt and pulled it free of his pants. Her hands skittered under his shirt and up his chest. He ground his hips against hers so that she could feel what she was doing to him.

"Up," was all she said as she tore her mouth from his before they slid across his cheek to his ear.

Thomas looked at the mountain of stairs before them— no way were they making it up there. With a little self-control, he slipped his hands out of her shirt and pulled out of her grasp that was as tight his. Turning her, he pushed her up the unbelievable number of stairs. As she went, he had a perfect view of her butt in the flowy skirt.

Just a few steps short of the landing, he couldn't keep his hands to himself anymore and slid his arms around her waist. His hands found her breasts again. Above him, she stopped and leaned back into his arms, pushing her still-covered breasts further into his hands.

"Three more," her amazingly husky voice said.

"Too far." His hands were pushing her bra over her breast, so he was finally touching her naked flesh, her pert nipples. Nipping at her neck gently with his teeth made her moan.

As she pulled away, his hands slid down from her breast

to her waist as he followed her up the last three steps to the top of the stairs. He looked past her blonde head at the tiny, short hallway with two doors, neither giving any indication they were hers. No longer caring, he pushed her into the wall, and his lips were on hers again.

Feeling her fingers on his shirt, he dragged his mouth from hers and grabbed the hem of her pink blouse and yanked it over her head, ignoring the buttons that should have been unfastened. Feasting his eyes on the purple bra he had been thinking about for so many hours, all he wanted now was for it to be gone.

Somehow, she had lowered the bra back over her breasts, but his lips wanted them, and he kissed down her body till he got the edge of the purple lace. His white shirt was on the ground with her pink one before he even knew what was happening, and her hands were pulling his T-shirt over his head. At that point, his mouth found hers again.

Running his hands down her hips, he slid her skirt down her legs. It fell away easily. As he made fast work of getting her naked, she was doing the same to him. He hissed at the sensation that ran through his body when her hands slid over his bare chest and down his stomach. Before he could think, her hand slipped into the waistband of his slacks, her fingers grazing the top of his hard erection.

So wrapped up in the feeling of her hand on him, he had stopped exploring hers, stopped everything as she carefully unsnapped and unzipped his pants. Then his cock was in her hot, little firm hand. It was all he could do to not come right there in the hallway.

Forcing his concentration back on her, he loved that she was in purple panties. Her body was pure perfection before him in the matching set, and what little imperfections she had just made her sexier. His finger traced the lace of the panties, and he felt her suck in a breath. Hooking his fingers around the lace, he pulled it down slowly.

On a breathy sigh, she demanded, "Make me come, Thomas."

"Say please, Kit." His eyes were on the newly exposed skin before him.

"Now, Thomas." Her hand slid slowly up and down his rock-hard cock.

Per her request, his fingers slipped insider her folds, and he was greatly rewarded with a moan as her head fell back, exposing the tender flesh of her neck. Taking advantage of it, his lips showered the skin with light kisses as his fingers did her bidding. He knew she was close when she was unable to hold on to his cock anymore and let go as she moaned in pleasure. Watching her climax almost brought his on, and would have if she were still holding him.

With her eyes still clouded, her breathing was still uneven when she said, "You had better have a condom on you."

Bending down, he pulled his wallet from his pants and opened it. She took the entire wallet from him. Pulling out three condoms, she looked up at him and innocently said, "Only three?"

Grabbing them all from her and the wallet, he threw down all but one and quickly opened it before sliding it on. Needing out of the hallway, he started pulling her toward him to go into the apartment, but she was having none of it as she stood her ground and dragged him back toward her.

"Now, Thomas. Please, now," she whispered

Groaning, he shifted her so that she was back against the wall, but this time, he lifted her slightly as her legs wrapped around him, and he slid easily inside her. Her warmth wrapping around him made him groan. He had been with many women in his life, but none had fit this perfectly to him.

Needing to catch his breath in order to make this last, he

buried his face in her breasts, but only then did he realize she still was in the sexy bra. He really liked that bra.

Thoughts of purple bras slipped from his mind as Kit's body demanded he move, and as the moaning sensations of her body wrapped around him, he finally met all her demands.

He was completely consumed by her body and the noises she made with each movement—her hands gripping his shoulders tight enough that he knew she would leave marks, her breathy pleas for more, and her blue eyes.

Her body clenched around his cock so hard that he couldn't stop his orgasm, didn't even want to. The spasms kept coming as his own orgasm hit hard.

Completely spent, he lowered her to her shaky feet and looked around the hallway again. They hadn't made it into the apartment or even within four feet of it. Their clothes were everywhere, and he was still wearing his pants around his ankles, and his shoes and socks. With her blonde hair a mess, she was only wearing that amazing bra that barely contained her breasts.

Not that any of that mattered since he had her in his arms. Naked in his arms. Even now he knew he should have wined and dined her to get to this spot, but he wouldn't change the last ten minutes for anything.

"You're pretty good at that." Pulling away from him, she leaned against the wall still behind her, her voice husky.

"You're not bad yourself." He drew her back into his arms, hating her being away from him, even if it was only by a foot.

"I do my part." She chuckled, pushing her hair behind her bare shoulder.

Slipping his hands behind her, he slid his hand up her back to her bra strap. "Let's get this off."

Her body fell back against the wall, pinning his hand so that he had to stop. "Can I leave it on?"

"Why?" He ran his free hand over the lace and slid his thumb over her covered nipple, starting to dislike the bra just a little.

Biting her lip, her breath caught as he did it again. "Please, Thomas, I just want it on."

"Okay." He used the hand behind her to pull her back to him. He left her bra on her as requested. He still loved it and would spend every Friday from here on out wondering if she was wearing it.

Pulling away from her, he pulled up his pants and gathered up her clothes as she opened the door to the apartment on the left. All that was on the door was a "2." Dropping the clothes as he entered the apartment, he pulled her back into his arms. He was not done with her yet. Not by a long way.

CHAPTER 5

IT HAD BEEN SO LONG since she had a man in her bed she didn't want to leave, ever. Even if it wasn't her bed, and the man in it would be gone the moment he realized she has kids —one of which had been crying for over an hour. It was just past four in the morning, and her mom, Dolly Nordskov, was throwing in the towel. James had won the battle of will between grandma and baby.

The text hadn't woken Thomas, but Kit was instantly awake when she heard the quiet buzz from the other room where her phone was, still in her skirt pocket. Climbing out of bed, she padded nearly naked to her clothes, hoping it was nothing. But of course, with five kids, a call in the middle of the night was never nothing. James was up and wanted his mom. Badly. In the back of her mind, she wondered if he knew she was having a good time without him, and it bothered the baby.

Dressing quickly, she texted her mom she was on her way. Pulling her shirt over the bra she still wore, she wondered what Thomas had thought when she wouldn't let him take it off. He felt them and caressed them, but there was no way she could let his lips on them. Her only thought as he had tried a few times to get it off was her breasts leaking all over them. James was still nursing, and she hadn't nursed him in hours. Right now, she was hurting with the need to feed him. Her night of single life was over; it was time to go back to being a mom. Back to being the Kit she became over a decade ago.

Looking down at the naked man who had made her body quiver and hum for hours, she regretted leaving. Checking her phone, she calculated the time but knew she had to get to her mom's place ASAP. No time for another around. Evidently, three rounds were not enough. Not nearly enough. She would happily go for a fourth, even though he was out of condoms. She knew there were more somewhere in this place—she knew her sister well. More importantly, she had an IUD, because there no way she was getting pregnant. Not again. After five kids, she was not taking chances.

His body was gorgeous, and she was happy to have been able to have touched every inch of it. Running her hand up his bare chest, she watched his eyes open sleepily. "Hey, you."

"I have to leave. You can stay, but Mandy could be home any time after six. Take the sheets off the bed before you leave and throw them in the laundry basket in the closet." She tapped his chest twice and walked away from him.

"Really?" he asked from the bed, gorgeous brown eyes on her.

Turning at the bedroom door, she took in his naked chest again. "Really."

Turning again, she walked out of her sister's apartment. If she stayed any longer, she wouldn't be leaving for a long time. Her mom had done her a great favor taking the kids, but her mom was over it now. If she didn't get back home soon, there would be no more leaving her kids with her parents for some time.

Thomas didn't say anything to try to stop her, and she was happy for that. Her resolve was getting weak, and it would've been easier to turn around than to leave. But he said nothing as she closed the door. Down the hallway, she wondered how there was no evidence of the hot explosive sex that had happened there just a few hours before. Shouldn't there be some burn marks in the old carpet at least?

Pushing those thoughts from her mind, she headed down the stairs, as far from Thomas as she could get. From the moment she saw him months before, she had known sex with him was going to be better than anyone she had been with before. And now he had destroyed her for anyone else for years to come. Many, many years.

On the short drive to her parents's house, she hoped her mom didn't notice the post-sex glow on her. Then chuckled, shaking her head; her mom never noticed the post-sex glow, hence JJ. Maybe if her mom had noticed the glow, she wouldn't have gotten pregnant early in senior year.

After she had left the rehearsal dinner yesterday alone, she had walked to the back of the cemetery to see Hanna's grave. She had visited a few years back, but only once. Now the past was so much on the surface that she had to see her name, just once.

Hanna Hazel May. Yes, her actual name, Hazel Hanna May was right next to it on the stone, with no end date listed since Hazel was still living. On the end was Henry John May, the boy. Always alphabetical. Kit hadn't known him well. He was just a kid who was in Jamie's class, then was Jamie's friend. But mostly he was one of the triplets, the boy.

It was midsummer when Jamie had brought Hanna around for the first time. They were going to babysit for her so that she could go out for the evening with friends. Even at that time, she could tell they were falling in love. Young love that might not last, but love. Jamie had a hard time with Jeff's death four years before, and Kit was happy he was finally starting to get out of his funk that summer.

After that night, they would both come when her lawn needed mowing or just when Jamie had time. They would take the three boys for rides in the car or walks to get them out of Kit's hair. It was heaven-sent for her. The kids were overwhelming at four, five, and six. And when they would come back, they would stay and watch TV or movies or just talk.

A few short months was all they had. If they had broken up that day, neither one would even really remember their time together. But they hadn't broken up, and she knew they weren't even thinking about that when they died. In fact, they were thinking the complete opposite of breaking up. They were planning a future together.

It had only been a week before that when two of them had come to her, Hanna in tears, Jamie very close. Hanna was pregnant, just like Kit had been so many years before. They wanted, needed, advice on what to do now. Hanna was afraid of what her grandparents would say, what Jamie's parents would say. What everyone would say.

Kit had given them the only advice she could: she had chosen marriage, but they didn't have to. There were other things that could be done. They had to choose what to do.

Squatting down, she touched the date of death on the stone in front of her. Three days before the cold date chiseled in stone, they had told her that they too wanted to marry and keep their baby. Kit had been excited to have a niece or nephew one day soon and would help them any way she could. Not that her life was going anywhere at that time. She had only five semesters of college done but had actually decided to take a hiatus that semester. After she had worked hard for so long to get her degree. To make her life better. Then she had given up again, admitting defeat once again.

But that night she had let them go out. It was a Friday, and they wanted to be young, so she let them be young before life started for them. Because life was starting sooner for them than for their classmates.

Over the years, she had never really talked to either of Hanna's friends. Not knowing if either Natalie or Hazel ever knew that Hanna was expecting. At first, she had wanted to tell them, tell them that Hanna had been looking forward to the future before it was stolen from her, but later she didn't want them to know if they didn't already know. What would it matter in the end if three died that day or four?

With a heavy heart, she had walked to the bar to get her last glass of booze for the evening while watching her sister's TV. Seeing Rafferty at the bar was what she needed. His happy-go-lucky attitude pulled her emotions from the floor. Over the years, she hadn't seen him much and loved seeing him again. For a long time, he had a crazy crush on her cousin, Mia. Kit had noticed it in high school and had made fun of him for it. And still did. Mia had never noticed, and he never did anything about it.

Then Thomas had walked over and took over her space and her thoughts. All the emotions swirling around her turned to just wanting him, to touch him, to get lost in him. She had fought off the thoughts as long as she could, but her emotions had won out, and she had dragged him to her sister's bed. Well, first her hallway, then her kitchen floor, and then her bed.

Pulling up to her parents's house, she pushed those feelings down deep. She was a mom of five and had no time for memories of Thomas's hands on her body, or her hands on his. It was a one and done anyway, something to get him out of her system. And he was out now … she hoped.

The door hadn't closed behind her before her mom had shoved James in her arms. His little face was red and covered in tears and snot, but he was still adorable. At six months, he was her baby, her last baby forever. When his dad had walked out on her before she even knew she was pregnant, she thought that Josiah was her last baby. Then a month later, she realized that there would be one more, James. Since her ex-husband didn't show up for his birth, Kit had named him after her dead brother-in-law, which just made her ex madder. Not mad enough to change it, but mad enough that he didn't really spend much time with his boys. That was until he had a girlfriend who was willing to take care of them for him.

Watching her mom leave the room, Kit brought her son to the living room and sat in the rocking chair, so she could watch the sun come up and nurse him. There was a bottle in the fridge she could feed him from, but she wanted the contact this morning more than anything. As the sky lightened to start another day, the baby quieted and snuggled close. With a full tummy, the infant slipped into sleep in her arms.

Closing her eyes, Kit knew there was no way she was going to the wedding now. She needed until Monday to come face to face with Thomas Harstad; in reality, she needed way more than until Monday. But until Monday was all she had.

CHAPTER 6

IT WAS COMPLETELY UNREAL. Kit was just walking out on him at four o'clock in the morning. Not even looking back at him as she did. Though she had given him a checklist of things he needed to do before he could leave. She was fully dressed as he had watched her walk out of the bedroom, leaving him alone and wanting her back.

With the click of the door to the apartment, he flopped back onto the bed, unable to suppress the grin of his face. Looking back on the evening, he realized he hadn't had sex that good in years, if ever. Kit knew what she wanted and was not afraid to tell him, and he had never been with a woman who took control like she did. He liked it.

He climbed out of the bed that she said was actually her sister's, pulling the sheets from it as he went since she had asked. Though she could have asked nicer. A lot nicer.

Tossing them in the laundry basket, he looked around the room. Last night he hadn't wasted time doing that. The place was nicer than he expected from a small-town apartment, and it was furnished cozily. It was exactly what he would have thought her sister's apartment looked like, from the little he knew her sister.

Not that he knew much about her sister, but he did learn a lot about the woman he had thought he already knew. And all the new information made him like her even more. In fact, he knew that he was going to ask her out, either at the wedding or the reception, both of which he planned to spend as much time as possible with her during.

Dressing in the living room, where his clothes were, he looked around the small apartment. It was comfortable. His eyes focused on the kitchen floor since that was where they had made love the second time. That was as far as they made it before he had to have her again, just a few short feet.

He looked around the room for pictures to see Kit one last time. Her sister had very few pictures of her family in the apartment and only one that was of Kit. In a snapshot on the fridge held on by a butterfly magnet was the four siblings. Two from the dinner the night before and Kit and another sister who looked so much like Kit they could be twins. It was an odd shot since Kit was wearing a flowing skirt, and the sister was wearing almost the exact outfit that Kit had worn to school on Friday. In one picture, he saw the two sides of Kit Kittson and knew that the one at school was not the real one.

The rest of the pictures on the fridge were snapshots of blonde kids in groups. They all looked almost identical, and all looked like the siblings. It seemed Kit's family made up more of the next generation than her brother's girlfriend's baby. Her sisters had been busy.

He took one last look over the apartment. He hoped her sister wouldn't see right away that they'd had sex in it. *Many times*, he thought as he shut the door behind him. It was something siblings didn't want to know about each other.

Once outside the door into the predawn light, he saw that

her bag was still there on the sidewalk. Smiling at the memory of her holding that bag so protectively, he picked it up. Maybe he would bring it to her on their first official date. With a new bounce to his step, he carried it with him to Ruston's house just a few blocks away.

As he walked, he marveled at the town. Had nobody even seen the bag, or had they just left it because it wasn't theirs? He would never know. But he really liked Ruston's little town with all its surprises. The best one being Kristiana Kittson.

As Thomas tried to sneak into the house, he found Ruston making coffee already. Putting Kit's bag on the counter, he took Ruston's cup and went and sat at the table.

Ruston was the first to speak. "You found someone in less than twelve hours?"

"I can't keep the ladies away, Rusty." Thomas smiled, taking his first sip of the hot liquid.

"Did you even try?" Ruston filled another cup and walked over and sat down at the table.

"I don't kiss and tell." He chuckled

"Yes, you do." Ruston set down his cup.

"You got a nice little town here. I was looking for my Hazel," he said, wondering if he had actually found her. The woman was fascinating and such a mystery.

"Did you find her?" He leaned back in his chair.

"We'll see what I can make of it." He told him the truth. Now that he had a taste, there was no way he was not going to see how far this would go. He just had to get her to finally say yes to a date.

"Good luck," Ruston stated without meaning it. Thomas had never thought about settling down with one woman, and Ruston had heard it time and time again.

"So here we are. You're marrying that crazy good singer you, well you know, met at a party. I'm not surprised you had it bad that night. If you had been able to find her, you would have married her that day." Thomas loved that Ruston had lost his usual control so much he had slept with a woman at a party, but in true Ruston fashion, he had fallen in love with her right then. And now was marrying that very woman.

"I maybe would have. I should have," he confirmed.

"Any doubts?" Thomas asked. He would have tons of doubts if it was him.

Of course, his buddy had doubts. He had asked the woman to marry him two weeks before, and they hadn't had a long easy relationship up to that day. Since it was Thomas's job, he listened to his friend and gave suggestions. Though he was sure that nothing he said was new to his friend. He knew more of what he was getting into than Thomas did. Ruston just needed to talk about the situation with someone. Thomas was usually that someone, but he was about to be replaced.

All the while, Ruston didn't ask any more questions about where he had been the night before. No probing, no prodding. The reason became obvious when the man's fiancé came walking out of his bedroom a few minutes later. Though he didn't know the woman much at all and what little he knew of her didn't say she was shy. But he loved that the woman his friend had chosen blushed when she saw Thomas as she left her fiancé's bedroom. She could have stayed hidden away from him, but instead, she walked out of the room as if she had done nothing wrong. Which to Thomas, she hadn't.

Drawing her into conversation, he couldn't suppress the grin when the petit woman who had just blushed at leaving the bedroom crawled onto Ruston's lap as they talked, proving once and for all to Thomas that this woman loved his friend just as deeply as Ruston loved her. Something that he was almost sure she hadn't realized yet.

As Ruston walked Hazel to the door after a text that she was needed back up town, Thomas grabbed his bag and went to take a shower. It was time to start the day. Waiting for the water to warm up, he regretted that he would be washing Kit's sent from his body, feeling it was over the minute he did. He also knew that was crazy since he was going to see her again today, hopefully all day until he was dancing with her in his arms at midnight. And hopefully beyond.

CHAPTER 7

IT WAS the post-sex high that got her through breakfast with four boys and her parents. Kit should have been as exhausted as the now sleeping James, but nope, she was fine. As the older boys settled in to watch TV and Josiah was happily sitting with her dad, she took a quick shower and put on jeans and an old T-shirt, her usual weekend attire.

With her hair in a ponytail, she bound down the hallway of her parents's little house, finally ready for the day. When she was growing up, they lived where her brother Math now lives, but seven years ago, when Math and his first wife Karen had gotten pregnant with baby number three, the older couple moved into a smaller house a few miles away, leaving that one to her brother's family.

Most weekends, as she waited for Brian to pick up the two little ones, she wished her parents had not been so generous with their only boy. Their new house was not built for eight. Since she had started at the school, she had been looking for a place in town for her and the kids. Though she rented in Grand Forks, she wanted to buy a place here. She spent every weekend here, all of her summers, and this is where her family was. To her, it made more sense that she bought something here, even if her job wasn't here.

Her mom saw her and shook her head. "You can't wear that to the wedding."

Stopping, she looked down in confusion at her jeans and Landstad Tigers shirt as if she hadn't just put it all on. Then shook her head at her mom. "I'm not going to the wedding."

It was what she had decided as she showered, as much as she wanted to see Thomas again. She couldn't. Shouldn't? *Wouldn't* was more like it. Best to stop the affair right now. Things could wait until Monday.

"Of course, you are, Kit." Dolly closed the dishwasher.

"I would have cleaned up, Mom." Kit saw that the kitchen was cleaned of the breakfast dishes.

"I'm happy to do it, Kit. I miss the mess sometimes," Dolly said with a smile. Her mom lied all the time like that. Kit was there every weekend with her, and her mom was cleaning up after them all the time. Kit always felt guilty and sadly relieved that things were getting done without her doing it all. But her mom shouldn't be doing it either.

"You do not, Mom. You were so happy when Julia finally went to college," Kit teased. For as long as Kit could remember, her mom was a mom. Her kids were everything to her. She had never had a job or many hobbies when the kids were at home. Dolly Nordskov raised kids.

"I should have had six like Dotty," her mom mumbled, not for the first time. Dotty was Dolly's little sister, and they lived within a few miles of each other. Both had married farmers and had kids, but Dotty had six to her mom's four. Kit knew that if Dolly hadn't stopped having kids before Dotty started that there would be seven Nordskov kids. Both sisters wanted to one up each other—Dotty had six just to have more than Dolly.

"You do not want six, Mom." Kit laughed. After all she had five, which was so close, she didn't wish that on anyone.

Now all the sisters seemed to do was argue about who had more grandkids. Dolly was ahead, but Dotty would win in the end. Dolly's kids were older, and two of Dotty's hadn't even started yet. Her cousin Mia being one of them. Kit had done her part with five, but her sister Mandy wouldn't have any due to medical issues. Dolly's kids were definitely on the wind down since Math was the only one having kids these days, and his girlfriend was nearly forty. And Dotty's youngest, Kipling, wasn't even twenty yet.

"You have to go get dressed for the wedding." Her mom pointed at her again.

"I'm not going to the wedding. The boys wouldn't handle it. They don't want to go to a wedding." It was her excuse, but she didn't want to see Thomas today. Or, more importantly, she didn't want Thomas to see her and her kids. No way was she hiding five kids from the man. Once he saw them, it would be over. It was only a one-night stand, and telling him about the kids was the easiest way to make sure it stayed that way.

"Dad will watch the big ones, and we can take the little ones." Dolly pointed to her husband watching TV with the kids. He was great with her boys. When she had been young, he had been busy farming and had little time for his own kids. In retirement, he had all the time in the world for any and all his grandkids. But not all of Kit's at once, alone. That much she knew.

"I barely know her," Kit pointed out and poured herself some coffee.

"You know him. And you have known her all your life," Dolly stated, as if it was a known fact.

"All her life. She's a lot younger than me." She wondered

how old Thomas was. She had never heard. His friend was marrying a woman six years younger than Kit. Her mom probably knew, but she wasn't asking.

"You know Hazel, Kit. Hazel," her mom said, as if Kit wasn't remembering all the good times she used to have with the woman, of which there were none.

"You go and take Dotty." Kit sat at the table.

"Mandy said that Hazel has almost no relatives. We get to sit on the family side in the front." Dolly sat down next to Kit, all excited about being considered family to a near stranger.

Oh good, even closer to Thomas. No hiding in the back. "Mom, I don't want to go."

"Didn't you have fun last night?" her mom questioned.

"I did." Kit took a sip of coffee, remembering the hours with Thomas. The rehearsal dinner itself wasn't the greatest. "But I don't need to see it."

"Mandy said it's going to be beautiful. Mandy and Mia worked very hard on it," Dolly protested.

Kit looked at her mom—her sister and cousin maybe did do some stuff for the wedding, but neither worked really hard on it.

"You would have to help me with the boys the entire time. Mandy is busy," Kit pointed out. It was usually Mandy who helped her with the kids during church.

Dolly looked at her over her coffee cup, and Kit looked right back. Instantly, her mom put her cup down, turned toward the living room, and yelled, "Otto, you have to watch the older boys, so Kit and I can go to the wedding!"

Kit didn't hear her father's response, but it was most likely an agreement. Dolly ruled this house, always had. So now she was going to this wedding, with just two kids, but that was enough to show Thomas things were over.

After lunch, Dolly finally got Kit into a wedding-appropriate outfit. This time the skirt was all yellow and the top was navy blue, but it was the same flowy material as the outfit the night before. Though she wore the skirts her sister gave her for work, they were not what she preferred to wear.

Then she changed the little boys into something other than sweatpants and t-shirts. At least she kept their church clothes in Landstad, so getting them wedding-ready was easy. Each boy got khaki pants and a white polo shirt. After having raised three boys for a while, she had learned to just dress them alike—it was easier. Once they were dressed, she took her time combing both their hair—what little they had so far.

Her mom stuck her head in the door, saying, "Dad wants to come, so get something for the big boys. He swears he will watch them."

Her mom retreated quickly, knowing Kit hadn't wanted to bring all her kids. Now they would all go. With James in her arms, she gathered up the same pants and polo shirts for the big boys. They were always called the big boys: JJ, Justin, and Jacob. At twelve, eleven, and ten, they were practically triplets. What one did, they all did. Though their personalities were very different, when together, they thought alike. Even though they could physically fight all day, they rarely picked on each other. She hoped her little two got along as well as the big ones.

Laying out the clothes, she went out and sent them all back to change themselves. Over the years, she had learned how to be in complete control over them. She didn't let them get out of hand, because if one did, they all did. It was the same as she controlled her classroom, where she was considered strict. But she didn't feel she was strict with her boys and instead made sure she hugged and kissed them as much as possible so that they knew they were loved.

With one arm around a chubby baby, she combed hair with the other, one blond head after another. Chuckling at the carbon copies of her that were her boys, she remembered her ex Brian's confidence that Josiah was going to look just like him. He had brown hair and brown eyes and looked absolutely nothing like either of the children he fathered. Even Jeff should have had genes to dominate the light blond, blue-eyed, pale skin, but they were not reflected in the kids he left behind. Some days she wished they did look like him. It had been ten years since she had seen her first love, and somedays she wanted the reminder.

Loading everyone into her SUV, she knew this was it. No way was she hiding this brood from the man conducting the service. But she needed to see the look of disgust in his brown eyes so she could stop seeing the desire in them.

Following her parents' Buick into town, she waited as they picked up Mandy from her apartment and then continued to the church. The big boys climbed out and took off to find friends as her dad followed them. He was in charge, after all—even if Kit knew the man would forget that the minute he found a friend to talk to.

Mandy helped get the little two out of their car seats and carried Josiah to the church. Kit carried baby James—sometimes she forgot she had him in her arms since she had carried so many babies. One day a few weeks before, she had started panicking when she couldn't find him. He was four months old, where could he have gone? Trying to control the panic, she had asked her oldest JJ to help her find the baby, at which point her first born had pointed out that she was holding him. Had been the entire time.

Inside the church, she wanted to switch with Mandy. James would be easier for her sister to control than the three-year-old. But for Kit's last two babies, Mandy had not been too keen on them when they were little. Only recently had she started to hold James, but maybe, "Mandy, do you want James? He's easier."

"I guess, if you want this one." Mandy nodded at the boy squirming in her arms.

"Yes. Here." They switched little boys and went separate ways. Mandy knew almost everyone and stopped to talk to them. Mandy was their mother all over again. Kit was more like her dad, who hated crowds. Looking around for a friendly face, she saw a classmate of Jeff's, Logan Tucker, who she hadn't seen in years.

"Logan?" Kit stated with a smile. He had grown up since he went away to college just as she started to have kids.

His hair was the same light brown it always had been, but now it was cut short while years before it had been halfway down his back. His green eyes looked at her from head to toe, and he smiled the lazy smile that landed him all the girls when he was in Jeff's band. "Kit Nordskov."

"How have you been?" She leaned in to give him a one-armed hug since the other had a boy.

"Good. You look amazing, Kit." Logan hugged her back.

"That's what a mom likes to hear, Logan. You were always the one with the smooth lines." Kit laughed. Though the man was gorgeous. She had always only had eyes for Jeff, and Logan still didn't do it for her.

"That's right, you and Jeff had two?"

"Three," she corrected him.

"I'm sorry I didn't make it back for the funeral. I was in school in Wisconsin." Logan's face showed the normal sadness everyone showed when talking about Jeff.

"To tell you the truth, I wouldn't have remembered if you were there. I was pretty numb for a long time," Kit responded, same as always.

"Who's this?" Logan pointed at the boy in her arms.

"Josiah. From my failed second marriage." She looked at the boy. "So, what are you doing now?"

"I'm VP at the bank," Logan said proudly.

"Really? I hadn't heard. Tess doesn't talk about work much. That and she probably doesn't even know we knew each other." Kit looked over the crowd for her future sister-in-law, the president at the bank.

Logan nodded slowly. "Tess is dating your brother. I didn't even put that together. When you're gone so long, you forget that everyone is related to everyone around here."

"Yes, for quite a few months now," Kit agreed.

"I was starting to think I wouldn't see you today." Thomas's voice came from behind her. She hadn't even noticed him approaching, and she had been watching.

"Thomas, you scared me." Kit turned away from Logan to look at Thomas. And man, he was just as hot dressed as not.

"Didn't mean to scare you, Kit." He said her name like he was still trying to get used to using it. No matter how much she had said it over and over again the night before. "Thomas Harstad." He stretched his hand to Logan.

"Logan Tucker." They eyed each other.

Men!

"Logan, this is Thomas. He's officiating the wedding today, and I work with him. Thomas, Logan and I went to high school together, and I haven't seen him in years."

They were still looking at each other like they were going to fight over her at any moment. And though she should be flattered, she was more annoyed than anything. Neither actually had a claim on her.

Shaking her head, Kit told them, "I have to go sit down."

Getting away from the men, she looked for any of her family members, who were supposed to be sitting in a certain area, but Kit didn't know where. Up the stairs to the sanctuary, she was disappointed none were sitting yet. How can so many blond people just vanish?

From behind her, she felt a hand go around her arm that wasn't holding on to Josiah. Turning, she was eye to eye with Thomas again, and he wasn't overly happy with her. He must already know. Well, she was holding one in her arms.

So captivated by his gaze, she didn't even notice when he pulled her into Pastor Ruston's office or when he shut the door. Her only thought was that she wanted him to kiss her again and never stop. Backing her into the wall, he did just that.

The kiss brought her back to the night before, and she moaned at her body's instant reaction. All she wanted to do was make love to him again and again. Her body pressed into his, but she couldn't get close enough.

A small groan escaped her when Thomas pulled away. It was only then that she felt a little hand on the back of her head. Noticing her son's other hand on the back of Thomas's pushing them together as if they needed more encouragement.

It seemed Thomas had finally noticed the boy in her arms for the first time, and he pulled away a little and looked at the little boy in the white polo shirt. Thomas dropped his arms from around her and tapped him lightly on the nose with his finger.

Josiah's expression said he wasn't very impressed.

"Who are you babysitting for today?" He didn't take his eyes off the boy.

"Nobody."

"Who is this then?" Running his hand over the blond hair, he looked into the blue eyes.

"This is Josiah. He's my son." She set her jaw at the admission, waiting for the reaction.

Thomas's eyes went straight to hers, then back to Josiah,

then back to her again. Now he had to see the resemblance that had been there the entire time.

"Where was he last night?" Thomas took a step back and demanded.

"My parents were watching them." She reached for the doorknob, needing out of this situation.

Thomas's jaw was set in anger, so Kit turned, opened the door, and walked out. That was easy but painful. Wouldn't it have been great to get another night from him before he rejected her? But that was not to be.

Mandy was coming up the stairs with James, and her eyes lit up when she saw her. "I have a meeting with the book club. I can't take him with."

Kit took her other son in her other arm. And now there were two. "Where are we sitting?"

Mandy looked into the sanctuary like she hadn't been there hundreds of times. "Fourth row, bride's side. I will send up whoever I see."

It was wonderful that her sister had friends now, something that Mandy usually struggled with. But right now, Kit hated that she was leaving her for them. Mandy had always been there for her, for the big things and the small things. Now she was leaving her for her friends.

Watching her sister hurry down the steps and out of sight, Kit felt alone. Turning, she walked into the church that was filling up.

Looking around, she saw some of the faces from the night before, but Thomas's sister, Ashley, was missing. Kit knew she was there, just not sitting down yet. Not that Ashley could help her; she had messed up with Thomas herself.

With a sigh, Kit sat where she was told to wait. Before long, her brother, Math, came and sat by her, pulling James to him. Then her parents came and sat on the end with her three older boys, all their hair in disarray. Math was lucky today—his ex had his kids, so it was just him and Tess.

By the time Thomas walked down the aisle to join the groom in the small room off the sanctuary, where every kid, who ever got confirmed at the church knew were the communion wine was kept, she knew she was going to miss it, even if she had barely had any of it.

CHAPTER 8

Foxy Kit had a kid. The entire time, she had a kid. A cute kid who looked just like her, but still a kid. Of course, she had a kid. After all, she was widowed and divorced. Who does both without having a kid?

He took calming breaths as he stood alone in Ruston's office, trying not to remember how her body felt under his. How she had just tasted with her kid in her arms. How he wanted her still, so badly, even with the kid.

For hours he had waited to see her again, see what she was going to wear today. Spotting her hugging some guy was not how he had thought he would see her for the first time after their night together. So, he had gone over there to remind her of their night together and let the guy know he had no chance with her—she was already taken.

As he walked through the crowd toward her, he had wondered how she always seemed to have a kid near her. Yesterday it was John Henry, and today it was this other kid. But he dismissed the thought. She was a nice woman who liked kids.

Following when she was certainly mad at him for intruding on her and the guy, he hadn't planned to pull her into the office. He had wanted to talk to her, but instead he had kissed her, and she had kissed him back. Until the kid touched him. He had forgotten about him.

Her kid.

Of course, it was her kid; he looked just like her. But so did every one of her siblings. Josiah. Cute name for a cute kid who had a sexy, gorgeous mother.

But Thomas didn't date mothers. That was his number one rule, always had been. He had been raised by an indifferent stepdad, so he didn't want to be one. He wanted his own kids or none at all. No matter how good that mother was in bed or how good she looked in navy blue with her blue eyes.

And where did she get all these skirts?

His watch told him that he needed to get to the front of the church, but his body was still thinking about having sex with a blonde mother, cursing the emphasis on "mother" in his mind. But she still looked good as a mother.

Out of the office, he headed down the aisle, and his eyes automatically went to the back of her head, her blonde waves sitting next to her brother. *Eyes on Jesus*, he commanded himself, looking at the painting on the altar and away from Kit.

Slipping into the room with Ruston, Thomas tried to banish all thoughts of blonds from his mind. But she wouldn't leave. Not that he had been successful in the last almost twenty-four hours of that.

"Where have you been?" Ruston was sitting on the edge of a table, looking like he was not scared to get married. Not scared to spend the rest of his life with one woman. Hell, he looked excited about it.

Shrugging, Thomas said, "Got distracted."

"Your lady from last night?" Nodding, Ruston smiled at him as if he knew exactly who Thomas was thinking about. Except there was no way.

"No. Hey, are you nervous about being a dad?" What was he even thinking? He didn't want to be that kid's dad, no matter who his mother was.

"No, I'm excited still. You already asked," Ruston pointed out.

"Sorry," Thomas mumbled. He knew why he was asking today—because Kit had a kid. He leaned back on the table beside his friend. He needed to stop thinking about Kit. "Are there going to be any nice single ladies around today?"

All he needed was a distraction. Another woman would be just what he needed to get his mind off Kit. Kit and her kid. Kit the mother. Kit the sexiest woman in this damn town.

"Nice ladies or ladies you would like?" Ruston asked with a smirk.

"Nice ladies." What was it with Ruston thinking the worst of him? Was he that bad of a person?

"Mia is single. Mandy is single, but Mandy is quite a bit older than you." Ruston looked at his watch as he said it.

"Mandy? Is she a Nordskov?" he asked with interest.

Not that he was interested in the woman herself. After all, he remembered her from the wedding. Not just because she was Kit's sister, but because she looked so much like Kit. That and she was the owner of the apartment he was in all night. An apartment he wouldn't soon forget.

"You said it right. Yes, she is. The oldest."

"What about the other sister?"

"You won't like her," Ruston stated, his smile gone completely.

Thomas gave a nervous laugh. "Why would I like the other sister, who is quite a bit older than me, but not the one closer to my age? What's the difference? One sister verses the other?"

"Because, Thomas, you are you. Everything you say you don't want, she has." Ruston straightened his tie.

"A kid?" Thomas needed the information to be reaffirmed for some reason that the kid was hers. As if Kit herself would lie to him. But he needed one more person to tell him she had a kid. Then it would sink in that she had a kid.

"Okay, let's see. She is older than you, she has not had an easy life, and she has kids," Ruston stated.

"Kids?" he choked out. What happened to one? One might have been OK. One could have been doable.

"*Kids*, Thomas. Three from her first marriage, and two from her second. I know you; you don't want that. So, leave her alone. Find whoever you were with last night and leave Kit alone."

Thomas had no response to that. Five kids were way more than one. Like five times more. Thinking back on their night together, he tried to find anything about her that screamed she'd carried five kids. Except for the bra thing, nothing came to mind.

All he wished for right now was to go back to the woman he had spent the night with last night, but she didn't exist. And she never had. But he already missed her.

A timer went off on Ruston's phone, and both men stood. Ruston said, "Now I get to marry her. Finally."

Both men walked out of the room, and Thomas was overwhelmed about how excited he was to marry these two people. He hoped there was someone who would make him feel half as happy as Ruston was right now. Maybe he would meet her soon and start their lives together.

Except he wasn't ready to settle down. In fact, he wasn't even looking for someone to settle down with. Just have a good time. Once things got serious, he was out. Since forever. Nothing had changed.

Five kids. That was a basketball team, ready-made.

Lifting his face to the audience, his eyes narrowed in on Kit Kittson. She was all he saw. And her blue eyes were on him; he couldn't see the color from where he was at, but he remembered every inch of her. The little boy was not in her arms, but she had a smaller boy pressed to her body and was rocking him gently.

As the bridesmaid and the groomsman came in, Thomas was not watching them at all but looking down the row of Nordskovs. Between the older couple were three half-grown kids in polo shirts, white like the little ones, looking exactly like Kit and her entire family.

The ceremony was short and the best one he had been to —never had he attended a wedding where the bride sang to her groom from her spot at the altar. And the groom, who was entirely captivated by his bride, couldn't concentrate on the ceremony. Never had he seen a groom so besotted with his bride, Thomas was glad they didn't have a long engagement. Ruston wouldn't have made it much longer than two weeks.

As he pronounces them Mr. and Mrs., he knew they would stay together until the end. No way were these two going to get tired of each other. It was a joy that he could be the one to marry them.

After watching the newly married couple walk down the aisle and out the double doors, his eyes landed back on Kit. They had landed on her many times during the ceremony. Sometimes he had to tear his eyes from her just to look at the happy couple. Her eyes had been on him every time he looked at her. Her arms had held the baby the entire time also. It hadn't taken him long to decide that all the children in the pew were hers. All her kids.

More than once, he looked them over in their matching outfits. Not a one had sat still for the wedding. But what growing boy would? The age span in the group made Thomas wonder exactly how Kit controlled them. Except he had seen her control twenty teenagers, so five little kids couldn't be any harder.

Watching her family file out of the pew, he decided he needed to talk to her. Though he had no idea why or what about. Maybe just to have her to affirm that the boys were hers.

He waited as the entire sanctuary emptied before he went down into the basement, where the reception was being held. Once there, he scanned the crowd. He saw her family at a table, but he didn't see her. Nor did he see any of her kids, not even one of them. Hiding them all in this crowd would be impossible. It would be like hiding a hockey team, minus the goalie.

"She left," Ruston said from behind him quietly.

"What are you talking about?" Thomas demanded, wondering why his friend had left his bride. He had assumed that Ruston would never leave her side again.

"Kit, she left.

"I'm not looking for her." Thomas folded his arms and checked the crowd again, this time tripping up at her sister before realizing Kit was gone.

"Okay, Thomas." Ruston slapped him on his back. "Don't you wish she had left her shoes behind?"

Ruston walked away, still laughing at his own joke. Hazel had left her shoes behind at the house party they had attended that Ruston had fallen in love with her at. No way was he in love with Kit Kittson, he just wanted back up her skirt. And now that he knew she had kids, he didn't even want that.

Five kids. Not enough for a baseball team, but far more than Thomas wanted to deal with every day.

CHAPTER 9

Sitting at her desk on Tuesday afternoon, Kit ate lunch alone as she corrected papers. Kit was sure most of these kids would be spending their lives yelling the wrong answer at the TV during jeopardy because they had no idea what happened before their births.

Perhaps she should talk to Sam Sullivan to see how he motivates his students. He was loved by all, unlike her, who was struggling with student popularity. Who would have thought the hardest part of teaching was going to be getting students to like you? Maybe if she hadn't slept with Thomas, he would help her with it. But that bridge was burned.

It had been a week, and she had yet to see him but in passing. Not that they saw each other much before, but then he would go out of his way to flirt with her. Those days were gone. The few times she had seen him, he had vanished quickly.

Picking up her phone, she checked her messages again. Most days, she wasn't able to not even look at her phone during the day, but this morning, Tess had gone into labor. Math's last text had been over an hour before, and she had been close. Kit assumed the baby was born, and her brother was too preoccupied to text. Since she couldn't go to the hospital until after school anyway, there was no need to text him for updates. That was their mom's job.

Seeing no new texts, she had just set the phone down when a noise from the hallway drew her attention. It was her lunch hour, and there should be no students in the hallway at this time. Getting up, she rushed to the hallway and saw two seniors fighting in the middle of the empty hallway. The two had been friends as far as she could tell, but something had changed that today.

Yelling the students's names, she tried to step between them, but neither boy seemed to notice her to stop punching each other, until one grabbed her and threw her to the ground. As she went down, she heard more teachers yelling, but when her head hit the cement floor lightly covered in stained carpet, her head started to ring, blocking out the sounds around her.

Laying stunned on the floor, she saw a few male teachers pulling the kids apart, then shoving them toward the principal's office. Though there were half a dozen other teachers there, it was Thomas who knelt beside her. Sitting up cautiously, she touched her head. The pain was intense.

"Are you OK?" He ran his fingers over her hair.

"Fine, just bumped my head a little." She straightened her shirt and skirt to make sure she was modest. Short skirts and teen fights didn't mix.

His fingers lingered before leaving her hair; whether it was the pain or the feeling of his touch, she pressed her hand to the same spot. He stood up from his crouch and offered her his hand. "What were you doing getting in the middle of them?"

Taking it, she let herself enjoy his touch again, if for just a moment. "I was trying to get them to stop."

"Don't do that again."

For a moment, she thought he was going to continue until she was in his arms. But as the electricity from his touch started up her arm, he dropped her hand as if she had hurt him.

"I'll try not to." She winced, and her hand went back to her head, which was now forming a bump.

His eyes locked on hers in the middle of the hallway, but with the ringing of the bell, the classrooms emptied, and she couldn't see him anymore. With nothing to do in the hallways, she turned and went back into her classroom, away from him. Cleaning off her desk, she watched as the juniors slowly filtered in.

Before putting her phone in her desk drawer, she checked it one more time, just in case. And of course, when she had been trying to break up a fight, her brother had finally texted. It was a girl, as Tess had been saying since the beginning. But now she was here.

After work, she would get to see the newest Nordskov baby and, happily, it wouldn't be hers. Sadly, it usually was.

A few hours later, the last of the seniors were out the door. All she had to do was get through the next thirty minutes, and she could head home. Her head was throbbing now, and she half wished she could leave, but she had to go see the baby today. Or be forced to explain her injury to her mother. That was not going to happen.

Sitting down in her chair, she decided to see if Math had taken any pictures yet. Her head was not impressed with the sitting idea, and she got up, taking her phone with her. Straightening the student chairs as she flipped through the dozens of pictures, she chuckled at her brother's picture-taking ability. There was a picture of the baby's hand and one of her thigh, maybe. One picture was just of Tess, no baby at all.

"Reading history jokes?" Thomas asked from the doorway he was leaning on and nodding at her phone.

Stopping, she turned and looked at him, not expecting him to talk to her. To even flirt with her a little. Despite the scene in the hallway, she hadn't expected to see him for another few days. She definitely hadn't thought he would never actually talk to her again.

"I wish. Just amazed at Math's inability to take pictures. Tess had the baby today, and he sent pictures, and some might not actually be of a baby." She started to move the desks again, trying to keep herself from pulling him into the room and having her way with him.

"Some people have problems with cameras." He didn't step into the room.

"Next time I will have to request that Tess take the pictures," she told him.

"Do you think there will be a next time?" he asked with a raised eyebrow.

"Oh, yeah. Tess's family is huge, so there's no way she'll stop with just one, even if Math has three already." Getting the last one in place, she went back to her desk and sat down.

Though Tess was almost forty, Kit was sure the couple would have at least one more. Her family was large, even bigger than hers. Just because she started late didn't mean she wouldn't have herself a few more. And Math would do anything and say yes to anything Tess wanted.

"Do you need pain relievers for your head?" Thomas pulled her thoughts back to him as he pushed off the door frame and walked her way.

"No, but thank you." She touched her head again, which was indeed still throbbing.

"Is it bothering you still?" He leaned against the same desk he had the afternoon before the wedding. Except this time, he wasn't looking down her shirt. He had already seen it and wasn't interested in a repeat.

"Yes, but I'm fine." Her eyes met his dark ones.

"Are all Nordskovs this stubborn?" His lip quirked in amusement.

"Yes, we are." She grinned at him. "I can't take those, Thomas."

"Can't or won't?" His eyebrow went up in question.

Leaning back in her chair, she looked in right in the eyes. "I shouldn't take them because I'm still breastfeeding my youngest. Mandy recommended that I avoid them if possible."

"I didn't realize." His eyes dropped to the floor in front of her desk.

"It's fine. By morning, it'll be alright," she explained.

"Seems a long way away," Thomas stated, eyes back on her.

"It is, but I've done it before." After five times, she was an expert.

"I suppose." He nodded.

"Thomas, I don't want everyone around here knowing about the boys. I like to keep my personal life personal." She said what she should have told him a week ago. She had half expected him to tell everyone Monday morning that she had a ton of kids. She was happy he didn't. She liked that nobody here talked about her, that the gossip was kept away from her and her kids.

"Yeah, sure. If that's what you want, Kit," Thomas agreed.

"Thank you, Thomas. But I have to go. Time to see if Tess can combat the Nordskov genes. So far, nobody has." She chuckled at her joke.

Without waiting for a response, she headed out the door. The day was over, but it was going to be a long, painful night.

One that she wasn't looking forward to. At least a few hours will be filled with new babies and family.

And maybe the pain in her head would keep her from thinking about Thomas late at night. Remembering his touch, his kisses, just everything him.

CHAPTER 10

THOMAS DIDN'T KNOW which Kit had kept him up longer: the one moaning in pain on the ground in the hallway or the one in another hallway moaning as she came in his arms. Between the two of them, he had gotten less sleep than he really needed.

Then there was the Kit, who was breastfeeding, which should have been a turn-off but made him long to see it. Knowing she was still breastfeeding was the reason she hadn't taken off her bra that night. Suddenly, he had more questions to ask her.

After a week of forcing himself to stay as far from her as possible, he had thought himself successful until the fight—a fight she got in the middle of despite the danger. He had almost thrown himself into the battle, except two of the gym teachers beat him to it, pulling the boys away from her.

Seeing her lying lifeless on the floor wasn't something he ever wanted to see. Instantly, he thought that he had lost her, that he had lost any chance with her. Not that he wanted a chance. He wasn't stepfather material, after all, and she still had five kids when she crumpled onto the dirty floor.

So, when she started to move, he could breathe again and push thoughts of losing her from his mind, thoughts of never-agains. All he could do was make sure she was alright.

But he couldn't stop himself from going to her classroom later to make sure she was OK. To make sure for himself that there had been no serious damage. To see her one more time.

Which was what he told himself as he watched her looking at her phone and moving the desks without knowing he was there. Again, she was in the knee-length skirt and a silky blouse of light blue, not the flowy skirts of the weekend. He liked her better in the long skirts, but he also liked that he could see her legs in the shorter ones. In reality, he had liked her in every outfit he had seen her in so far.

Leaning against the door jamb this morning, he watched as she corrected papers with a red pen. Nothing out of the ordinary, but he couldn't take his eyes off her. Couldn't stop himself from talking to her, despite all the reasons not to. "How was the baby?"

Startled, she looked up at him, then smiled. "Tess has nothing on Math's genes."

"Math's genes look pretty good on a girl." Pushing off the wall, he walked into her room.

"Smooth, Harstad," she said with a grin.

"I try." He shrugged. "Did they name the baby yet?"

"No, they're in a standoff over it. Neither are ready to budge yet."

"Who's going to give in?" he asked, loving that she was far more relaxed and didn't seem in pain this morning.

"I don't know yet. Tess is stubborn, but I don't know if she can beat Nordskov stubbornness." She smiled.

Ginning at her words, he joked, "Ah, the famed Nordskov stubbornness raises its head again."

"It's one of the things we're known for." She set her pen down and leaned back in her chair.

"What's another?" He wanted to know anything about her. Everything.

"We don't tan, just burn." She shrugged and looked at her bare pale arm.

"Any others?" Enjoying her openness today, he wanted to know more.

Shaking her head again, she grinned and admitted, "No, we're perfect other than that."

"Modest too."

"Yes, we are. It's part of the perfection." Picking up the pen, she toyed with it as she looked at him.

"Ruston called and said that book club is going to see the baby tonight, so I have John Henry and Ruston to entertain." Since the man didn't get to town much and from now on rarely without his family, Thomas was happy to get to spend time with his friend.

"That should be fun. How is the happy couple?" she asked, though her smile wasn't as bright as before bringing Hazel into the conversation.

"Great was what he said." Thomas watched her set her pen down.

She looked up at him, and he could tell her smile was different. "I could see he's besotted."

"Oh, he is. How well do you know Hazel?" he asked.

"Not well. She's six years younger than me, so we didn't run in the same circles." Her eyes darted to the farthest corner of the room. Was she lying to him? Why?

He knew that everyone in town knew everyone else and that nobody was actually a stranger. But it seemed there was something more to it than that. They attended the same church every week. Kit's sister was close with Hazel. But Kit actively seemed to avoid her. Even at the wedding events they were at together, neither spoke more than a few words to the other.

Hazel had lost her brother and sister in an accident years before, and Kit had lost her husband in an accident. Maybe that was the reason behind their distance.

"What do you know about the accident?" he asked. She was from the town, and everyone knew about the accident. Ruston had said Hazel was still not over it.

Before his eyes, her face grew pale, and her gaze dropped to her desk. Instantly, he wished he hadn't asked.

"Enough, I guess." She looked intently at the paper in front of her.

"Okay, just asking." He shrugged, not pushing.

"My, um, brother-in-law died in it. He was dating Hanna. That was Hazel's sister." Her voice was shaky, and she didn't look up.

His heart hurt for her. She lost so many people she loved over the years. "I'm really sorry, Kit. I wouldn't have brought it up if I knew."

"It's OK." She looked up and gave him a weak smile of reassurance. "Most people don't remember. Jeff, my husband, his brother, had been dead for a few years already when it happened."

As the morning bell rang, interrupting their conversation, he looked into her eyes and saw the pain that still was there over her losses. Getting up, he put a hand on her shoulder and said, "If you want to talk about it, I'm available."

"That's OK. It was years ago." Brushing him off, she stood up and turned her back to him to get something off the table behind her desk.

Watching her, he knew she wasn't over the incident but knew she would never talk to him about it. Now she knew that he knew, but she was also saying she didn't want to talk about it with him. And he was assuming it wasn't just him she wasn't talking about. That she was just burying it, letting it fester.

Over the course of the day, he tried to catch Kit to talk about it. He had no idea what he would say, but the pain was still there after six years. And probably compounded by the fact that her first husband had died in a car accident years before that.

Passing by her classroom at the end of the day, he saw she was already gone. Heading to his car, he wondered if she had taken the day off. Would she take the day off after talking to him for five minutes about her brother-in-law, but not when she had an untreatable headache the day before?

At 6:00 p.m., Hazel dropped off Ruston and John Henry for their man's night, or man's few hours. To Thomas's surprise, Sam Sullivan joined them since he and his girl-friend had ridden with Hazel and Ruston. Thomas took them to a popular restaurant in town. The place was busy and maybe too loud for a little boy, not that Thomas was paying attention to that sort of thing. In the end, John Henry seemed to be doing OK.

Even though they had seen each other less than two weeks before, they had a lot of catching up to do. After rehashing the wedding for a few minutes, Ruston asked, "Did you ever call that woman from the dance?"

Thomas looked at him. What woman? The only woman he was interested in was Kit, and she wasn't at the dance. In confusion he admitted, "No."

"You should. You'll like her. Everyone likes her," Ruston stated about the woman Thomas couldn't even remember.

"I don't remember her."

"Brunette, shorter," Sam stated. He must know who Ruston was talking about.

"Nope." He shook his head.

"Still hung up on Kit then?" Ruston laughed.

"No, she's just a coworker," he said firmly. He wasn't hung up on her; she was just all he thought about these days.

"Wait! You work with her? You never said anything about that," Ruston questioned.

"You never asked," he said, even if Ruston would have had no way of knowing it.

"I've always gotten along with her. She's a nice woman. You two would make a nice couple," Sam piped in.

"We only work together. Not a couple," Thomas restated, in case they had forgotten they were just coworkers.

"How about the kids thing? And she's older than you," Ruston pointed out, reminding him of his list of things he didn't want in a woman. As if he could forget.

"We're not dating; we just talk. At work. Because we work together." Thomas was not admitting to anything.

"Okay, I'll drop it. For now. Can I tell Hazel yet?" Ruston asked with an eyebrow wiggle.

"There's nothing to tell." Because there wasn't, and there never would be.

"So you keep saying," Ruston teased.

"I will definitely not tell Natalie, or the entire town will know. I know my woman well." Sam chuckled at his own outgoing fiancé.

Their meals came, and they all dug into the food before them, and conversation stopped almost completely. Thomas watched his friend help his new son eat. John Henry seemed to become distracted easily, but Ruston got him back on task. Thomas wondered if all kids were like that or, more specifically, if Kit's kids were.

"What do you know about the accident?" Thomas asked. Since it had bothered Kit so much to talk about earlier today, he wanted to know more about it without asking her.

"What accident?" Ruston asked in confusion.

"Hazel's," Thomas said, though Hazel wasn't even in the accident. But everyone at the table knew exactly what he was talking about.

"Not a lot, but enough. I know more about the fallout after than the actual accident itself. It messed her up pretty good for a long time. Messed up a lot of people. Why?" Ruston put down his silverware.

"Kit's brother-in-law was in the accident," he admitted.

"I guess she was a Smith, and he was a Smith. I never made the connection before. I wonder if Hazel remembers? I don't think she would have let her watch John Henry for the wedding if she had. She distances herself from everyone in the accident." Ruston leaned back in the booth.

"Everyone involved does, guys. I was there that night. I was part of the volunteer fire department then. I saw it, I try not to think about it. I understand where both of them are coming from on this. Natalie has the scars that show, others do not," Sam remarked as a text came that they would be picked up soon.

"I think Kit does too. But I don't know if many people remember." Thomas remembered the interaction she had with Natalie Beckett the night of the rehearsal dinner and how she nearly broke down when she heard him call Kit a Smith.

The men were quiet for a minute before a text came saying that the women were ready to leave town. Which meant all conversation was over as they got their coats on. It was just as well; it wasn't their issue to deal with.

But he knew that each of them had a woman in their lives that had been profusely affected by that accident. That none of them were over it, and years hadn't dulled the pain.

He didn't know what he was going to do to help Kit, but he knew he wanted to. Wanted to do everything in his power to help her, with anything and everything.

CHAPTER 11

THE THREE DAYS of school before Thanksgiving should just be canceled.

Kit's students were paying no attention to what she was saying anyway. All that was on their minds was a four-day weekend. It was utmost in her mind also, but she pushed through it.

As the last bell of the day sounded, Kit almost cheered. Finally. Not that it mattered, there were two more days like this before her favorite holiday. It hadn't always been her favorite—Christmas had always held that spot until she was a poor single mother of three. That was the holiday where your mom feeds you, and you don't have to buy anything to take prominence in her heart. Adding two more kids hadn't changed that.

The seniors filed out quickly, and she tried not to take it to heart that they hadn't seemed to enjoy their hours with her. But she knew most didn't.

Walking through the classroom, she straightened the desks that were completely out of line and wondered if Thomas would swing by her classroom today. She really enjoyed it when he did. Not that she would ever admit it out loud.

Last week he had even started harmlessly flirting again. Oddly it was more fun now since she flirted back, and they both knew it was going nowhere. Now he knew she had kids, so he wasn't interested in her in that way.

But it was fun to be seen as sexy, even for a minute or two a day. It was also nice to have someone to talk to who knew her family and that she had kids. She had even realized how much she missed being able to just talk to someone.

"How was your weekend?" came the sexy voice from the doorway that sent shivers up her spine. She wished it wouldn't, but it did.

Turning to him with a smile, he was looking fine in his gray slacks and white sweater. "Good, I helped Mom get ready for the holiday. Julia is coming with her girls."

"Julia?" he questioned, folding his sexy arms.

"My sister." Then she laughed. "The other one. She's younger than me."

"The one that looks like you?" he asked.

Taken aback, she had no idea how he knew Julia, and they looked more alike than she and Mandy did. Sure, everyone in town did and could have told him, but had anyone? "How did you know she looked like me?"

"One, because you all look the same, and two, I saw a picture of all you kids on the fridge at your sister's apartment." He tried to suppress a grin. They hadn't talked about that night before. At all.

"Oh, OK." She concentrated on the desks for a moment, not on the memories of what had happened in that apartment. "Julia lives in Fargo and doesn't come home much. Her husband is odd."

"You don't like him?" Thomas stepped into the room.

"No, never have. But she's happy, so I don't say anything."

Getting the last desk straight, she headed back to her own desk in the front of the room, walking maybe closer to Thomas than she needed to. But she needed to be close to him for a moment.

"I'm glad my sister married Randy. I like him." He didn't move as she brushed past him.

"But you're closer to Ruston?" Smiling, she questioned him, pausing for a second in front of him.

"Yes. Randy was way more into sports than either of us. So, we became close, and he found other friends. But he was there for Ashley when she needed someone." His hand reached out and brushed her hip before she walked away.

"What happened to her?" She walked to her desk, wishing she hadn't moved.

"Got messed up with the wrong guy for a while. It was worse than she ever told me about. Or anyone except Randy. He figured it out, and they fell in love. Or she fell in love. He had been in love with her for years already, or so he said." Staying by the door, he smiled at his words.

"They seem happy." The little she had seen of them, she would have said they were truly happy.

"You talked at the rehearsal dinner, didn't you?"

"Yes. We chatted."

"I bet she knows everything about you. She's evil that way." Thomas laughed at his sister.

"She did seem a little evil, but I was raised with three just like her. I have to go. Kids to pick up." She organized her desk for the night, though it was basically clean. She just wanted to spend more time with him.

Nodding, he said, "Sure, you are busy."

"My work is never done." Desk clean, she grabbed her coat from the cabinet and slipped it on.

"I can't even imagine. Do you always go to Landstad on the weekends? Ruston said you were a member of his congregation," Thomas asked as he watched her button the coat.

"Almost everyone. Brian, my ex, is supposed to get the boys, the little two, every weekend. He doesn't usually, but if I don't bring them out there, he could take them away from me. Not that I think he ever will, but I don't take chances." It was one reason. The other was that she loved her hometown and really wanted to live there full time. Life just got in the way.

"Not a happy separation?" he asked.

"Happy for him. He found his way into the bed of a twenty-year-old for a few months. Of course, I got rid of him to an unsuspecting child, so happy for me too." Grinning, she grabbed a stack of folders from a project her class was working on, a project that wasn't going as planned.

Though the woman Brian had left her for was long gone, she had been easy to replace over and over again. Kit wasn't the only fool to fall for him. It happened all the time. Even during their short marriage.

"His loss," Thomas said quietly, almost too quiet for her to hear.

Kit looked at him quizzically but let it go. No need to push something that wasn't going anywhere. All too soon, Thomas would find someone else to turn his attention to. All too soon, she would be forgotten.

With that on her mind, she headed out. He followed, but they separated in the hallway, going in two different directions. Just like in life.

CHAPTER 12

Did she really need the folder?

Probably not.

He had found it ten minutes after she left in the hallway. Instantly, he knew it was from the stack she had been carrying when she left. It had to be. He was just as sure it was important. That she would need it tonight.

Charming her address from the school secretary should have been harder than it was. Far harder than just spending ten minutes with the woman, talking about sports and the weather. But it worked in his favor, so he was OK with it.

He looked up at her two-story little twin home that had her SUV in front of it. The house didn't look big enough to hold her and five boys, but it must. It was almost six, and the air was chilly today. Winter had arrived, even if there wasn't any snow yet.

At the front door, he knocked, still wanting to turn and run away. Why was he even here? What was he going to say?

The door swung open, and a blond boy with Kit's blue eyes looked at him in question. The kid didn't say anything, just looked at him in the open doorway.

"Is your mom home? She forgot these at work, and I thought that she might need them," he overexplained to the kid who probably didn't care.

At his words, the kid turned and yelled into the house, "Mom, someone at the door for you."

Then he turned and walked away. His job was done. Thomas caught the door before it could close and took a step inside. It was warm and tiny inside, but there was no clutter, no mess that kids created. Five kids, in fact.

"Who is it, JJ?" Her voice came from somewhere in the house.

"I don't know!" the boy yelled at her as he flopped onto the couch.

Thomas nearly laughed at the kid. He was no help to his busy mom. He was in no way going out of his way to help her.

"I'll be out in a minute. Keep them company," her voice said.

"OK," said the boy, who just looked over at him but didn't get up.

Thomas smiled at the kid who didn't smile back, and the two other identical sets of eyes looked at him. None made a move to make him feel comfortable or even welcome, just out of place. Which just made him want to leave. There was no need to stay.

Except, she was here.

"So, you are JJ. What are your brothers's names?" He pointed at the other two on the couch. He didn't know any of their names but Josiah. Yup, he one hundred percent remembered the kid's name. He had it bad for this woman.

"Justin and Jacob," JJ provided, but didn't point out which was which, so he was still lost as to who the kids were.

"Who's oldest?" He wanted to see if he could get the others to talk, because JJ was not very helpful.

"I'm." JJ pointed to himself and smiled.

"Who's youngest then?" Thomas had no idea since they all looked the same age.

"James is," JJ answered again. But James had not been the names he had already given. Thomas assumed it was the baby's name, who would obviously be the youngest.

"Where do you go to school?" He wondered why she didn't send them to where she worked. Though both of them worked in the high school, there was also a middle and elementary school. And a discount to teachers on tuition.

"Kennedy," JJ said with pride.

Thomas looked around the house and wondered what she was doing that she couldn't stop for a minute. How much more small talk could he do with the kids?

"Sorry I kept you waiting." She came down the stairs when he had been sure she was in the kitchen. It was closed off to the rest of the house, so he had been sure she had been there.

After seeing her in so many skirts, he was surprised she was wearing black leggings and an oversized gray T-shirt. In her arms was the baby she held during the wedding. He was happy and making all kinds of baby noises. Her eyes widened in surprise when she saw him standing there. "Thomas, what are you doing here?"

"You dropped this. Thought you might need it." He held up the folder for her to see his excuse for being here.

Her eyes were on the file. "It wasn't that important for you to waste time bringing it to me. You could have just brought it to me in the morning."

"I didn't know," was all he could think to say, because all the effort it had taken to get there was all worth it to see her one more time today.

"Well, you're here now. Have you eaten?" Maybe she was

as happy to see him. Because so far, she hadn't kicked him out the door.

"No," he answered honestly.

"I have a tater tot hot dish in the oven if you're interested." Her eyes were watching him closely. It was a test, and he knew it.

A test he was going to pass, he decided as he took his coat off.

"Sure."

"Boys, go wash up for supper," she called to the kids on the couch.

Thomas watched the three jump up from the couch and take off in a herd toward the back of the house. Kit walked over to the couch they had been sitting on and pulled a toddler into her other arm. Now she was carrying both the little two, but both were staring at him with concern.

"Can I take one?" He nodded at the boys.

"I doubt it. They've never seen you before," Kit stated. She carried them into the kitchen as if she did it all the time, which she probably did.

Following behind her, he realized she looked pretty good in leggings. This was the first time he had ever even seen her in pants. Watching as she dropped one into a booster chair but kept the baby in her arms, he knew she had done this same routine over and over.

As the older boys came to the table, they fought and annoyed each other. Until their mother scolded them, then they sat quietly and ate. Kit calmly fed the three-year-old with the baby on her lap and let Thomas control the conversation with the other boys. He found out they were at the public school and all played soccer, but each wanted to play something else. Their mom said no. He learned that they were all around a year apart in age and all had birthdays in June. That their dad was dead, and they never saw their other grandparents. But every weekend, they went to see Kit's parents.

And since they were kids, he learned that Kit's ex never took advantage of his visitation rights unless he had a girlfriend to watch the kids. But that the babies never liked to leave Kit. He learned that their mom never dated. Ever.

By the time they went to watch TV, Thomas thought Kit had been embarrassed enough by her children. She was trying to coax another bite into the little guy, who was done eating, but she was mostly just avoiding looking his way.

"Kids don't understand secrets." With the open space, he slid closer to her.

"I had too many with big mouths." She tossed the spoon on the plate she had been trying to feed the boy with, then put her head in her hands.

"You're the one who chose them." He pointed out with a grin.

"No, no. I was using protection for each and every one of them." Getting up, she took the older boy to the kitchen with her.

"That does not bode well for me." His smile faulted. They had sex and used protection.

Not that he had minded the kids tonight; in fact, he had enjoyed spending time with them. More than he had ever expected he would. After a while, he hadn't even noticed that there were so many. They all were different and fit together as a cohesive group.

"You'll be fine." She washed the boy's face and put him down to run off. "I have an IUD. Not going for number six. I'm done."

"Good to know." He released the littlest one from the highchair and picked him up. He was happy the boy didn't seem to mind him holding him. And even happier that he didn't have to worry about one of his own of these little guys.

"So why are you here?" She leaned against the counter, letting him keep holding the little boy.

"You forgot a folder. I left it by the door." He tried to make it seem more important than it was. And he knew he was failing.

"Why are you really here, Thomas?" Her eyes bored into him at the question.

"To spend more time with you. Even if you have a ton of these." He pointed at the boy in his arms.

"They're always here. I don't get days off from being a mom. Jeff is dead, and Brian is a deadbeat. There'll be no fun dates, just you and me. No weekends without them. Forever."

"I can't seem to convince myself to not be here." He leaned down to kiss her. "I want to see where this goes."

"I want that, too, but I'm worried that it'll get to be too much for you." Kit's arms went around his waist and pulled him closer, though there was a baby between them.

"Me too. Tell me that they at least sleep?" He pulled his lips from hers.

"Not this one, but the others do. In a few hours." She lifted the baby from his arms.

With a shake of his head, he took the boy back and headed for the living room. She had just said she never gets a moment away from the kids. Except he was there, and he was going to make sure she had time to herself.

Besides, if he was really going to do this, he was going to go in both feet first. Right now.

CHAPTER 13

KIT GRADED tests in the kitchen and tried to keep James entertained. She could have brought him to Thomas, but the other four were with him. No need to overwhelm him. They were watching a cartoon action movie. The boys liked to talk during the movie and were always moving around, which was why she hated watching movies with them.

She had expected him to bolt for the door hours before. Her boys were very well behaved, but they were still boys. They liked to do what boys do, and it seemed having a man in the house made them want to do boy things even more. And louder.

Before the movie was over, she switched little boys and took Josiah to bed. Since Thomas was there, Josiah didn't want to go to sleep, so it took an extra-long time. But once he was down, she had the older ones go up, and she followed. Once she had those down, it would just be one more, and he didn't have sensitive ears.

Teeth brushed and outfits picked out for tomorrow, she tucked them in and headed downstairs. They were pretty good about listening to her, and she would be back up to check on them soon.

Back downstairs, Thomas was talking to the baby in a low voice, and James was watching him as if Thomas was the center of the baby's world. Then James reached out and grabbed Thomas's dark hair, messing it up with his wet fingers. The sound of Thomas's laugh melted her heart. Maybe he could change his mind about kids. She could only hope he could change his mind.

"They're in bed but not asleep." She sat down next to him, already exhausted.

"How long?" His arm went around her and pulled her close as James crawled onto her lap.

"If I knew, I would put them to bed then." She let herself melt into him.

"You're very good with them. You almost predict what they're going to do next." He picked up the toy James had tossed.

"I should be able to. I've been doing this alone for as long as I can remember." She couldn't even remember a time she wasn't putting a baby to bed in the evening.

"And not one was planned?" he asked.

"Nope. Two led to marriages, and two were a little too close after the previous ones."

"You mean three birthdays in June."

"There are four. This one is the only one that isn't. He was born six months after my divorce. Brian didn't even show up for the birth, so he's mine." Hugging the baby close to her, she kissed the top of his head.

"Aren't they all yours?" He pulled her tighter to him.

"You can't prove that any of them are mine." She laughed because they all looked just like her.

"When did your first husband die?" he asked quietly.

"Just after Christmas, when Jacob was seven months old. He's the youngest of the three. He lost control of his car on the ice and hit the ditch. Died immediately. We'd been together for almost seven years." She didn't know if he knew any of that information. It wasn't something she liked to talk about.

"How old were you?" he asked.

"It will be ten years this year. I was twenty." It was a big anniversary for her. Not a happy one, but she had already lived through the wedding anniversaries she spent alone.

"With three little kids. No wonder you make it all look so easy."

"It's not. I'm tired all the time. I could sleep right now." She closed her eyes and exaggerated a snore for him.

"I'll go check the kids then." He kissed her head.

"No, I will. They'll just get excited if they see you." She patted his leg as she got up.

"I just hope their mother does." He smiled at her.

"She might even stay awake for it." She laughed and went up to check on the boys.

To her surprise, they were all asleep. Grabbing a diaper and pajamas for James, she went back downstairs. While she had been gone, Thomas had turned off most of the lights in the house, but he was still carrying James around. He was carrying the boy like he did it every day.

"They're asleep." Now she was nervous. With the boys asleep, they were as close to being alone as they had been since the night before the wedding. School didn't count because the building was full of people.

"Now what?' he asked, walking up to her.

"I don't know," she admitted. She had never been here before. A man in her house and almost all her kids asleep.

"Can I stay?' He cupped her cheek in his hand.

"Do you even want to?" She didn't know why; he was

already here and had been for hours. Five kids hadn't scared him off.

"Yes, Kit, I want to." His lips touched hers again, just as soft and light as in the kitchen earlier.

"We still have one to go." Pulling away from him, she held up the diaper and pajamas.

"What do we do with him?" Thomas bounced the baby on his hip.

"Change, feed, and he should fall asleep." She took him from Thomas.

"Down here or upstairs?" Tucking a lock of hair behind her ear, he looked at the stairway.

"Upstairs maybe." She turned and went quietly up the stairs, knowing he was following her by the squeak of the steps, but she didn't dare look behind her.

In her bedroom, she put James on the bed and tried to control her nerves. This was crazy. She wasn't this nervous when they slept together during the wedding weekend. But suddenly her bedroom seemed less adult and more mommish. And far more personal than her sister's apartment.

Flipping James over, she changed his clothes and diaper. Now in his blue pajamas, he rolled back on his stomach. He was not ready for bed, but he was usually up another hour.

"Is it weird being in my bedroom? With my kid?" she asked, sitting down on the bed.

"Not as much as I thought it would be," he admitted, sitting down on the opposite side of the bed.

"Sorry I didn't tell you about the children." She touched James's little hand.

"Why did you hit on me that day?" He touched her hand that had just touched the little hand.

"Because you're such a flirt, and you deserved a turn-around." She chuckled, remembering his cocky attitude that day and how satisfying it had been to turn the tables on him.

"It was crazy, and then I was suddenly seeing you in everyone. Which turned out to be true because they were all your relatives."

"How you ended up at the wedding I was at in Landstad …" she lamented, her attention on her son.

"Of all the weddings, you had to walk into mine." Reaching over, he brushed a lock of hair off her cheek.

"You mean Hazel's wedding." She touched James's back lightly.

"Do you think about your brother-in-law a lot?" he quietly asked.

"Sometimes. A lot of the time, I just think that he's out there living somewhere else. Like he went to college and just doesn't come home ever. But he is still out there. Sometimes I pretend that Hazel is Hanna, and she must be visiting her grandparents. It's stupid, but it helps."

"You were close with Hazel's twin?" he asked.

"At the end. They had been dating a while, and he would bring her over to spend time with the boys. I didn't go to her funeral. I feel bad about that. I should have gone." Over the years, it had been her greatest regret that she hadn't been brave enough to just walk into that church for an hour.

Taking her hand in his, he squeezed it. "You were dealing with a lot then also."

"But I was the adult. I should have acted like it. I feel guilty." Kit had no idea why she was even telling him about this.

"Nobody even noticed you weren't there," Thomas pointed out.

Grabbing up the baby, she said, "I have to go feed him."

"Don't change your routine on my account, Kit." His hand on her hip held her to the bed gently.

"I'm not feeding him in front of you, you pervert." Pulling away, she smiled, though she wouldn't mind doing just what he was asking. But not tonight. Tonight, she was far too nervous having him around.

"You want to." He pulled her back toward him.

"No, I will go feed him and come back." Running her fingers through his dark hair, she knew she wouldn't be able to say no to him forever about this. But it wasn't as sexy as he assumed it was.

Leaving him in her bedroom alone was somewhat exciting. To know there was a man in her bed, waiting for her. Something that she hadn't let herself admit she had missed over the last few years. Even Brian hadn't been close to as attentive as Thomas was. Not even in the beginning.

To her delight and absolute fear, James fell asleep faster than he had ever done before. Like he knew that his mom was nervous and could use the time it took to get him to sleep. Nope, instantly sleeping.

Up the stairs, she laid James in his bed, then stiffened her spin and went to hers. Thomas was sitting against the headboard, looking at his phone, still completely dressed in the shirt and slacks he had worn to school that morning. When she walked in, he looked up and smiled at her. That smile made her knees weak.

Setting his phone on the nightstand, he hopped out of bed and pulled her into his arms, his mouth instantly finding hers as if he had been waiting all night for this moment. Which he probably had.

So had she.

Warm hands slid under her shirt and cupped her breasts. The night they had been together, she had missed how good a man's hands on your breasts could be. Tonight, she promised herself that was going to happen.

"No bra?" he questioned with a grin.

"Baby is fed," she admitted. "That night, I hadn't fed him in a while. Could have turned embarrassing."

"Me getting complete control of your breasts could be embarrassing. Like a twelve-year-old boy embarrassing." He lifted the shirt over her head, admiring the breast he was talking about.

"I have a twelve-year-old boy." She scrunched up her nose at the images in her head.

He ran his hands over her breast to her hips. Then snagged her pants and pushed them down her legs. "I don't even believe that. They must have been adopted. Your body is too perfect to have had kids already."

"Thomas." She tried to stop him, mostly from talking about her kids while having sex with her.

"Kit, admit it, you're gorgeous. I can barely keep my hands off you on a good day. Today isn't a good day." Dipping his head, he ran his tongue over her nipple, making her moan.

"Thomas, stop talking and take me, please," she begged.

"My pleasure." He picked her up and tossed her onto the bed.

Quickly, he followed and reminded her how pleasurable being with him was. Every time.

CHAPTER 14

IT WAS Friday of thanksgiving weekend, and Thomas had convinced Ruston to invite him and Kit over for supper. He hadn't seen her since Wednesday in school, and he missed her. He had only woken up beside her twice and already missed her when she wasn't there first thing in the morning. He even missed the morning chaos that was her house before school. One morning, he had even let her go for a run and not distract her with sex.

Thanksgiving had been spent with his parents, then he had gone over to see Ruston's parents because his sister and brother-in-law did. The house was in disarray, and Hazel seemed a little nervous about the crowd, but she was pushing through. Thomas loved that she was willing to do things to make Ruston happy. And John Henry was loving all the kids.

At Ruston's mom's house, he had told Ruston about his devious plan to see Kit during the long weekend. Just see her, maybe touch her, and with luck, a small kiss. He had talked to her as she drove home the previous day, and this morning, she had called him from her bedroom before her mom decided she needed help. They were acting like teenagers who couldn't get enough of each other, but neither had mentioned taking the other to their family's holiday. It was too early for that. Neither felt ready to let their families into their relationship.

That was why he was on Ruston's front step, waiting for her as he watched a few cars that weren't hers drive by. What had his life come to that he was waiting on a woman to come to him. In the cold, no less. That she had kids upon kids, and he didn't care. They were good kids who made her who she was today. Without them, her personality wouldn't be hers.

When her large SUV finally pulled up to the curb, Thomas jumped to his feet and went to the driveway to greet her. It had been so long. When she got out of the car, he pulled her into his arms for a kiss. No way he wasn't kissing her immediately.

"Really, Thomas, I haven't told my mother yet." She pushed him away from her and looked around the neighborhood.

"Are you hiding me, Kristiana?" He looked up and down the street also.

"Yes. You do not want my family questioning your intentions." She opened the back door and pulled out Josiah. Then she handed him to Thomas. "I brought Josiah and James. Josiah is close to John Henry's age, so I thought they would have fun together. The rest are with my parents for the night."

He took the boy, who was no longer scared of him. The boys were quick to warm up to him. Actually, all five boys seemed to be OK with him. Not one had said anything about him being at their house constantly since he showed up with that folder. "What did you tell your mom you were doing?"

"At Mandy's. She'll cover for me if Mom asks," she confessed, though he already knew that. After all, getting her away from her family with no questions asked wasn't as easy as he had originally thought.

"Mandy won't question my intentions?"

"Mandy? Maybe, but that's fine. She owes me one." Kit grabbed a bag from the floor of the SUV.

"Why?" He hadn't heard that the sisters had any issues.

"Because this morning, she was a witch to me for no reason. It wrecked our family fun time," Kit said as she walked into the house.

"Sorry to hear that." Thomas barely got in as Ruston took the car seat from Kit's hands.

The entire exchange had been so natural. Why did it seem like he had been doing this forever with her? When had they even gotten to the point that this was routine? It had only been a few days.

"Welcome, Kit," Ruston said as he opened the door to let them in the house.

But the man gave Thomas a knowing look. A very knowing look. But with Kit with him, Thomas didn't care.

"Thank you for inviting me. I only brought the little two. I thought John Henry would like to have a friend. You invited the right person to have a playmate for him." Kit took the boy from Thomas's arms and took off his little blue jacket.

"That's not why you were invited, Kit. It was all Thomas's doing," Hazel said from the kitchen doorway, not quite part of the group. Thomas hoped she would warm up to the company before the end of the night.

"It did have the stink of him on it." Kit laughed. He let her have it because she was here.

"I have no stink," Thomas mumbled, frowning at Kit.

"Hi, Hazel." Kit put Josiah down. Over the last few days, Thomas had found out that Josiah had never met someone he was scared of. He was her most outgoing son. Without any hesitation at all, he headed to the toys on the floor in the living room. John Henry watched him beeline for the toys and just stared for a second before heading there also.

"Hi, Kit," Hazel said, not moving from her spot, her eyes more on the kids than the adults.

Ruston had removed James from his seat and held on to him. Thomas was sure Ruston was ready to have another child with his new bride, though he was sure the bride wasn't there yet.

"I can take James." Thomas reached for the baby and took him, somehow possessive of the baby boy. But he wasn't going to think about that. He was going to just enjoy his time with Kit.

Maybe by the end of the night, he would be able to get her alone. Because he missed her. It had been two days, and he had missed her. He had even missed her kids.

He had it bad.

CHAPTER 15

"Is there anything I can help you with?" Kit forced herself to ask. If this was going to work out with Thomas, she would be spending time with Hazel. They couldn't be the reason the men lost the connection they had. They could get over this.

Taking a step back and making Kit feel slightly unwelcome, she said, "No, it's ready if you guys are."

After getting everyone situated and the kids' plates filled, Hazel spent more of the conversation apologizing for not having another highchair than participating in the conversation. Not having the chair didn't bother Kit, but her continued apologies about it did. Didn't she realize this was hard for Kit too? That day didn't only affect Hazel.

Conversation flowed around general topics: local sports, Thomas and Kit's school, the kids, the church. Mostly the women didn't participate. Each attended to their respective children and ignored that the other was at the table, pretending that the other wasn't even there.

By the end of the meal, Kit regretted ever saying yes to Thomas about this. Being alone with Hazel was turning out to be as awkward as she had thought it was going to be.

Even with Thomas's hand on her leg, she was nervous and edgy.

It seemed that either the men didn't feel the tension or didn't care because they talked as if the women weren't even there. Only when Thomas took Josiah from her lap did he even look her way.

So, when Ruston decided that the men would clean the table and that the women should just relax, Kit wanted to scream. Why would he think that they would get along better together with nothing to do?

That was how Kit ended up sitting awkwardly on the same couch as Hazel May with nothing to do but watch their kids play. At least they got along and didn't seem to fight like some toddlers did.

With James between them and what little small talk there was used up during the meal, Kit tried to come up with something to say, anything to say. After all, she was older and should be better at this.

"So, you and Thomas?" Hazel said before Kit could think of something.

"I guess. It hasn't been long, though. We're still taking it day by day. I'm sure he will bolt soon. My kids are a lot to take on." Kit pointed at the one crawling on the couch.

Hazel smirked. "Ruston says that he's never seen Thomas like this. He says it's cute."

"I'm not putting a lot on it. It'll last for a while, then he will find someone else. I mean, they're the same age, and you're a baby compared to me." They were in far too different stages of life for things to last very long.

"You have a lot of reasons it won't last. Anything on ways it will?" Hazel asked, picking up James and setting him on her lap.

"Not a one. But I plan to enjoy it while I can," Kit confided, hoping the baby won't get scared and cry.

"Will you have any trouble at work if they found out?" the woman asked more to the baby as she tickled him, making him laugh.

"No, you just can't live in sin. Or at least let on to the students that you are," Kit told her.

"That's how it is with Ruston's job also." Hazel looked at the kitchen where the men still were.

"That's what Mandy said." Kit nodded.

"What is going on with Mandy? She's not as Mandy as she used to be." Hazel set James on the floor at her feet.

"It's the season. She gets depressed during the holidays. Has for years. I didn't know if she would this year since she moved back here," Kit explained, realizing it was the first Christmas her sister would spend in Landstad after moving home. Or maybe, more importantly, the first with her new friends.

Hazel smiled sadly and looked at the baby still close to her feet. "Thanks for telling me. I've been concerned for a bit. I could tell there was something wrong."

"She loves book club, and she has close friends now because of it. When she lived in Grand Forks, she had me, but not many friends, except those she worked with. Now she has all of you," Kit said, wishing her sister still lived near her. Missing her being just down the street instead of miles away, but still happy she was here and happy with friends. Or once the holidays were over, she would snap out of her funk and be happy.

Again, they had run out of something to say. Though they knew far more of the same people; it just seemed awkward to start talking about everyone. So instead, they sat watching the boys play until they started to fight a little, then Hazel had John Henry bring Josiah to his room to see more toys.

Kit grasped at something to say. "The wedding was beautiful."

"Thank you. I didn't have a lot to do with it. Natalie did almost all of it." Hazel shrugged as they watched John Henry give all his toys to Josiah.

"I didn't realize you two were friends until that weekend." Kit willed her son to stop taking all the toys from his new friend. To be a nice boy and share.

"We're not really. Natalie is just pushy," Hazel explained, her eyes on the boys and the toys.

James was between them and moving around on the floor, and Kit picked him up and put him on the couch again. He was just getting the hang of crawling, but he didn't like to leave his mom's side yet. And with it getting later, he was getting more tired. Thus, clingier.

"I never really knew Natalie—when I lived here, I mean." Kit picked up James and put him on her lap.

"She's different than she was, but some things are pure Natalie, and nothing can change it," Hazel said with a little chuckle.

"I remember she used to get in trouble a lot. I was glad that Jamie didn't hang out with her much back then." Kit cursed herself for saying his name. Why couldn't she just not talk about him?

"We used to get in trouble for following her also. I had forgotten you were related to Jamie," Hazel said quietly, her body suddenly stiff.

"He was Jeff's brother. Jeff was my husband," she explained. Jeff had been gone a long time now. If it wasn't for the kids, she wondered if people would even remember they had been married.

"I should have gone to his funeral, but we really weren't close. Even now I can't picture him unless I see a photo. Odd since we went to school all twelve years together," Hazel said, biting her lip nervously.

Kit knew she had said far too much. They weren't ready

for a regular conversation, much less one about the accident. The one subject they were both desperately trying to ignore.

"Our brains do tricks to keep us from losing everything. Most of the time, I just let myself believe he went to college and never came back. That he's married and happy elsewhere." Kit looked at her son tossing trucks across the room, being full-on naughty now.

"I like that. I wish I had done that." Hazel was looking at her hands intently.

"No, it isn't. Because it's not real, and it still hurts when you are actually reminded of that." Kit tried to control her emotions. This was hard.

"I suppose," was all Hazel said.

"Sorry I didn't go to Hanna's funeral. I told myself I was too busy with everything, but it was a lie. I should have gone." Kit finally said what she had needed to say for years.

"Did you even know her? I know she and Jamie dated for a while, but not that long." Hazel finally looked up at her.

"They used to come over and help me with the boys. My bigger ones were around Josiah's age then. With three, I could use any help I could get." Kit wished she was brave enough to just tell her more. How much she liked her sister and was happy she made Jamie happy.

Hazel sighed. "She never said anything, but we weren't close in the end."

"I wish you had been. I don't know if she was as close to Natalie in those days either. I think they were focusing on their boyfriends more than each other. That happens as you grow up; you lose focus on the important things."

"I had never thought about that. I always thought that she and Natalie were together when I wasn't with them." Hazel suddenly was interested in what the boys were doing. Very interested.

"Maybe I'm wrong. I mean, they were together that night.

Maybe they were always all together," Kit admitted, not wanting to have Hazel think she didn't know them. They were her friends, after all. "Hazel, I knew that they were drinking that night. I knew that they drank a lot, but I didn't stop them. I wish I had stopped them."

"You couldn't stop them. Nobody could. You have nothing to be sorry for." Despite her words, her jaw was set in anger.

"I've always felt guilty about it. I was an adult," Kit admitted, knowing Hazel's anger was well placed.

"I knew they were drinking that night too," Hazel said, her back stiff again, and Kit knew she was angry.

"But you were a kid." Kit said, knowing she could have stopped them when Hazel couldn't have. It was her duty as an adult.

"And you had no control over them either," Hazel hissed and jumped to her feet. Whether her intent was to stop the boys from fighting or to just stop the conversation, Kit wasn't sure. But either way, Kit had to get herself and her kids away from here.

Pulling her youngest into her arms, she mumbled her excuses as she put on his coat before snapping him into his car seat. Then she called Josiah to her and put on his coat with the same speed. Being a mom to five made dressing them a cinch. Grabbing the diaper bag, she knew she was running. She knew she should just stay and be an adult for Thomas, but she couldn't do it. She knew that her relationship with Hazel would always be strained. The past was too close for any real friendship between them.

Which meant that any future for her and Thomas was impossible. They couldn't be in a relationship if his friends hated her. And she wasn't going to be the cause of him losing his best friend.

She was already out the door and heading to her car, one

boy on her hip and one in his seat, both crying, when Thomas caught up with her. He tried to take Josiah from her, but she held him tight to her.

"You OK, Kit?" he asked, trying to take the car seat from her hand.

"Yes, of course I'm." Kit laughed it off as she opened the back door of her SUV.

"What happened?" he demanded as she snapped the car seat into place.

Ignoring his tone, she slammed the door and carried Josiah around the car. "Nothing, Thomas. The kids are just ready to leave. It's late."

Quickly, she put him in his car seat and shut the door, finally distancing herself from the crying boys. At least for a moment. The drive home wasn't going to be very peaceful.

"I'm going to call you later." He followed her around the car again, this time to the driver's door.

"Thomas, this isn't going to work." She turned to him, letting the words circling around her head out. It was true; she couldn't do this again, and staying with him meant she would be doing it over and over again.

Thomas gaped at her and grabbed her arm. "Kit, can we talk about this."

"No, Thomas, we cannot. You are friends with Ruston, but I cannot be friends with Hazel. I cannot do that." She pulled her arm from his hand and opened her car door.

"This isn't over, Kit," Thomas said as she got into her SUV.

Not able to look at him, she started the SUV and backed out of Ruston's driveway. Her eyes were on Thomas. He wasn't happy like he had been when they had arrived, but neither was she. Reality had found its way into their relationship, showing how much they didn't belong together. Never had.

She was halfway to her parents before she realized she had forgotten her coat. In her rush from the house, she hadn't even noticed. But now, as the boys cried from the back seat, she shivered at the cold air in the vehicle. Or maybe it was from ending her relationship with Thomas. Why hadn't she said no to him becoming a part of her life? Even now she wanted him there, but she wasn't going to be his biggest regret. And her coming between him and his best friend would cause that to happen. If not today, then soon.

CHAPTER 16

STOMPING back into his best friend's house, Thomas controlled the urge to demand Hazel tell him what had happened. What had she said to Kit? And it took everything in him. The evening had been going well until they were alone. At this point, he didn't know the woman enough to confront her about it. And if he did, it would destroy his closest friendship.

"Did you get to say goodbye to your girlfriend?" Ruston teased him.

"Shut up, Ruston," Thomas said, trying not to get into it.

"Come on, Thomas, can't you take a joke?" Ruston asked, though he was starting to see that Thomas was not in a joking mood.

"A joke, Rusty? She ended it, OK?" He grabbed his jacket he hadn't time to put on after she left. As he pulled it from the hook, he realized hers was there also. Forgotten.

"Wait, Thomas." Ruston followed him out the door into the cold.

Without looking back at his friend, he said, "No, I just want to get out of here."

He wished he knew where her parents lived, wished he could follow her. Demand she tell him what had happened so he could fix it. Because it had to be fixable.

"What did she say? Hazel said they were having a pleasant conversation," Ruston stated, as if they had time to go over every moment of the conversation.

"Kit didn't really think so. She said she can't be friends with your wife." He turned on his friend, though it wasn't his fault.

"Why?" Hazel asked from the doorway, her arms wrapped around her body. Whether it was because of the cold or to protect herself, he didn't know. And he didn't care right then.

"Because of the accident, I assume. It wasn't just you effected by that day, Hazel. Others got hurt." Thomas slammed his hand into the door he had just come in.

"I know that. I swear I didn't say anything," Hazel stated innocently, but Thomas wasn't buying it.

"Thomas, leave her alone." Ruston blocked her from Thomas with his body. It was then that Thomas realized she was shaking. He didn't care at that moment.

"Don't worry, I will leave her alone." Thomas slammed out of the house into the cold night.

Climbing into his truck, he couldn't not speed away from Ruston's house. He headed the same direction Kit had gone. But there was no way he would find her.

Instead of driving around aimlessly looking for her, he went home. He had been driving through the dark roads for over an hour and was still pissed off at Ruston and Hazel. But he was pissed at himself also. He should never have made her go over there. He knew the two women had a history. He knew that the two women didn't actually get along.

Now he had pushed her away, thinking that the two women would get over whatever was hanging between them if they just had a little encouragement. Thinking that his career training made him an expert on fixing people.

Parking his truck in front of his apartment, he just sat there, unable to move. As the cold night crept over him, he tried to see this from her perspective, asking himself why she seemed to blame herself for this accident? Where was the guilt coming from?

Was it not the accident that claimed her brother-in-law's life that had her feeling overwhelming guilt? Could that just be a cover for another guilt? An older guilt? A guilt about her husband's death years before that?

As much as she talked about the accident that took Jamie's life, she had never spoke in anything but vague explanations of Jeff's death. Not once had she said how his death had made her feel, how it had affected her, how she had dealt with it.

Jamie's death was all she talked about. That it was her fault they were drinking, driving, being kids. When nobody else even thought that—not even Hazel or Natalie thought that she was to blame.

Picking up his phone in the cold dark cab of his pickup, he called Sam Sullivan, a number he had gotten and never thought he would ever use. But he needed to talk to someone involved. And he knew one person who might talk to him.

Without looking at the time, he dialed the number. Sam picked up on the second ring, something he himself wouldn't do for an unknown number. "Sam, this is Thomas Harstad. Could I talk to Natalie for a second?"

"It's almost midnight, Thomas," Sam said, not handing the phone over.

"I know, it's important. Please. It won't take long," he begged. It was all he had.

"Since she is up, fine." Same handed the phone over to his fiancé.

"Thomas?" Natalie asked tentatively.

"Natalie, I need to ask you something, and I hate myself for asking. I want to tell you not to answer if you don't want to, but I want to know. No, I *need* to know."

"Ask away."

"Where did you get the alcohol that night?" he asked, because the alcohol was what caused the accident.

"That night?" Natalie's words came out faint, and he didn't know if she was questioning which night.

Thomas controlled his anger and asked with the same voice he spoke to the teens that came to see him, "Please, if you remember."

"So, uhm," she started, and he was sure she wasn't going to say anymore. But after a few moments, she added, "Henry always got the alcohol. There was a girl who liked him whose dad owned a bar in Campbell. She took the alcohol from the bar for him when he asked. That was how we got the tequila. There was a keg at the party that night."

"So, Jamie didn't bring the alcohol?" He had to ask, needing to be reassured it hadn't been Kit. Just in case she had forgotten.

"No, never. He, uh, wasn't even drunk that I know of. He didn't drink like the rest of us. Something about his brother drinking and driving years before," Natalie said quietly into the phone.

"Jeff?" he asked, though he knew there was only one brother. Kit's husband.

"Yes. I never saw him drink more than a sip or two of anything. Mostly he didn't go to parties. But when he started dating Hanna, he started to go with us. His brother was married to Kit. You should ask her about him. Oh wait, that would be awkward with you two dating. Former spouses are probably off-limits," Natalie said, then made some noise he couldn't identify and didn't know if he wanted to. "I'm going to call Mia."

Before he could question her, he heard her dialing. She must have forgotten that she hadn't hung up on him yet. Just when he was about to hang up, it rang. Within a ring, another woman was saying hello, and the two were having a conversation.

"Hey, Mia, how did Jeff Smith die? Do you remember?" Natalie asked her friend.

Thomas wondered if she had forgotten she hadn't hung up on him. Or maybe she wanted him to hear the answer. Maybe she knew he needed to know.

"Of course, I do. I was eighteen, and I knew him. Since he was married to my cousin, I know everything," Mia said. Of course, she was Kit's cousin, though he didn't know that until right then.

"Then tell us," Natalie demanded.

"Wait, who is us?" Mia asked in confusion.

"Thomas is on the line. He wanted to know," Natalie explained.

"Thomas who?" Mia, it seemed, had forgotten him as fast as he had forgotten her at the wedding. Which made him feel a little better about not calling her.

"You know, Ruston's friend Thomas, from the wedding. He's kind of dating Kit. Don't tell anyone. Kit doesn't want her mom to know. I figured you already knew, though."

Mia made a noise and said, "Why am I out of the loop? Why don't my cousins tell me things anymore?"

"Mia, back on track, please," Natalie begged her friend.

Mia paused for a moment and then said, "OK, hello Thomas. Jeff died in a one-car roll-over on his way back from a gig with his band. He had one almost every weekend. The band was iffy at best, but they were willing to travel, so they were booked here and there. That night he was drunk when the car crashed. Well, he was always drunk by the time midnight rolled around. At the time, the cops said there was ice on the road, but there might not have been ice at all. Kit would never believe there was no ice. Or that he was drinking, even if she knew he drank."

"But you believe it?" Thomas asked, wanting to know what the gossip was.

"Oh yeah, and it's not a rumor. He had a problem with it." Not answering about the ice, Mia went right for the drinking.

"But he wasn't twenty-one, was he? She wasn't," Natalie asked. Thomas hadn't realized she was still on the line, she had been so silent.

"No, he wasn't. Soon, but not yet," Mia said, and Thomas knew she was shaking her head as she spoke.

"How did he get the alcohol?" He asked the same question as he asked Natalie, only this time he was going to get the answer he didn't want.

"Kit worked at the Landing back then," Mia said in a near whisper. It wasn't a rumor she wanted to spread.

The words made Thomas's heart sink. Of course, she blamed herself for his death. She was getting him the alcohol to fuel his habit. Even if she didn't get him the booze, he drank that night. She had been getting him alcohol for a long time. And she saw herself as the one to blame for the accident that took his life.

Mumbling his thanks, he hung up on the women. He knew everything he needed to. Way more than he wanted to. Kit was blaming herself for Jamie's death because she was already carrying the blame for Jeff's. Why hadn't he seen it that way from the beginning?

CHAPTER 17

AFTER SPENDING an hour watching Hazel Abbot throughout church on Sunday, Kit knew she had to talk to her. Not for either of them—they had gone this long avoiding each other and could go the rest of their lives easily. But for the sake of the men they loved, they had to talk.

Kit hadn't even made it back to her parents' place before she realized why Hazel had bothered her so much. It was because Hazel had found happiness, a happiness that Hanna would never have. But it was completely unfair to the woman who had no control over that night.

Turning back to town, she left the kids finally sleeping in the car as she walked once again into the cemetery, but this time, she went to the other side of the church. To where Jamie and Jeff were. This was the side she never went to, to be reminded of them both taken so young.

As she looked down at the two headstones, she couldn't read what was on them in the dark, but she didn't need to. It was all trapped in her memory, and she couldn't escape it.

Except Hazel's words were ringing in her head. She couldn't have stopped it. Nobody could have stopped it.

There was no way to go back and stop it, and there was no way to fix it. All that was left was letting go of the guilt and start living. To live when they couldn't.

Hazel was doing that. She had lost the two people closest to her since birth. But now she was moving forward, creating a life with Ruston and her son. Letting go of the anger and pain.

Natalie had also started to move on with her life, though she would carry the scars with her forever. A constant reminder that she lived, and they didn't. That she was special enough to live.

Kit wanted to move on also, to move past the pain and guilt. To not be consumed with the knowledge that she was to blame. And why was she to blame? She hadn't given them alcohol; she hadn't forced them to drive fast down a gravel road or even at all. How was she to blame for something she hadn't even been close to? She had been home with her kids. Sleeping.

Sinking into the hard dead grass, she felt chilled to the bone as she looked at Jamie's grave. Pushing past it, she remembered the happy kid she knew, the one who lived life to the fullest. The one who stopped at her place so excited because his crush since forever had said yes to a date. The one who was so excited to be a dad, more than his brother had ever been at the same prospect.

No, she wasn't thinking about Jeff tonight. She wasn't ready to go there. Because it was easier to remember the good times and the fun they had. Though as the years past, she remembered fewer and fewer of them. Some of the bad times had snuck into her memories, times she had wanted to forget.

With tears in her eyes, she headed back to her parents' house, swearing she would talk to Hazel at church one more time. Because she wanted more than remembered happy times, she wanted a future of happy times. Happy times with Thomas. And there would be none of those without his friendship with Ruston.

Now, as she watched Hazel slip out of the church, she knew she had missed her opportunity. That this had to happen today, or it would never happen at all. Somehow there was a time limit on this, and the longer she put it off, the less likely she would get herself to do it.

Without talking to Ruston, in case he just stopped her, she grabbed Josiah and left the other boys with her mom and Mandy. They could handle them until she got back. She had more important things to do today.

Walking across the lawn, she forced all doubt from her mind. She had to get this over with or lose Thomas forever, and she couldn't do that. Not now.

Without knocking, she walked into the house. Yup, she was a bitch.

Stepping into the house, she said, "Ruston said you were probably at home. Josiah wanted to say hi, and I couldn't get him to stop."

"I think John Henry was feeling the same." Hazel sat up from the couch, quickly wiping the tears from her face, pretending they were never there.

"Are you OK?" Kit lingered by the open door, letting the cold air into the warm house. She was unsure if she should keep it open or closed or just run away.

"Fine. I'm fine," Hazel stated, getting to her feet.

"Can we talk?" Kit asked and took another step inside, shutting the door behind her. If the door had stayed open much longer, she was sure she would've bolted.

Before she could say anything, Hazel replied, "Kit, I want you to give Thomas another chance. Everyone can see how much he likes you and how good he is with your kids. I think you two could be really happy together."

"Thomas and I have a lot of obstacles in our way." Kit took another few steps toward the couch.

"I'm not going to be one of them. I know I'm a reminder of the past, but I'm leaving. I swear, Thomas and Ruston can be friends again. I won't get in the way of that." Tears were in her eyes again, making Kit feel even worse.

"What are you talking about? Where would you go?"

"Away. Ruston is tired of John Henry and me. I'm not worth it. He realized it the other night. He and Thomas have been friends forever, and he doesn't want to lose that. Not for me." Hazel ran her sleeve over her eyes and sat back down on the couch.

"You mean the same Ruston who told me that I was Thomas's Hazel?" It was weird at the time, and still was a little weird, but it had warmed her heart just the same.

"I knew he would get tired of me. I thought I had more time." Her words were quiet, like she didn't want Kit to hear them.

Kit sat down across from her on the coffee table. "Did you know that I knew that Thomas was going to a wedding the same night I was in October? He said his best friend was marrying the love of his life and that he had been in love with her since the summer. I knew there was no way we were going to the same wedding. After all, you had only been engaged for a few weeks. Whirlwind courtship and all. I never imagined he would be at your wedding."

"He only married me to save his job. It was either that or leave Landstad. A permanent mark on his record." Hazel's tears just got bigger as she admitted it.

"Thomas told me he lied to you to get you to marry him. That he was so afraid of losing you, he lied to you. The Ruston I watched marry you wanted to marry you. He was so in love with you he couldn't think straight that day." Kit looked at her and smiled. "For a man who had officiated hundreds of weddings, he messed up the vows three times. That says something about how distracted he was by you."

"Why would he lie to me?" She wiped her eyes again.

"Because you are stubborn and would have left town if he hadn't. He didn't want to live without you. And I'm starting to understand what he feels." The last she didn't want to admit to her. She wasn't exactly ready to tell Thomas she had feelings for him, and definitely not anyone else.

"But I'm not worth anything, I have no job and no skills," she whispered.

"You were always the most talented of you three. Hanna told me once she thought you would be a music star one day. She was going to be your manager," Kit admitted, wondering if Hanna had ever said anything like that to her sister before her death. Or if she just told others how proud she was of her. Letting her sister never hear the words that she needed to hear.

Hazel sniffed and asked, "When did she say that?"

"The summer before." Kit didn't have to say more; they both knew when before was.

"They were always so much smarter than me." She shook her head in disbelief.

"You saw them that way. Henry may have been smart, but Hanna was struggling with school. They were not as perfect as you remember them being. With them passing, we were all able to paint them in a better light." Kits realized it was how she saw Jeff. So perfect in death it had made him perfect in life. Except she knew differently.

"You didn't know them," Hazel argued.

Kit paused. Hazel was right; she didn't know them well. "I knew Hanna. Maybe not as well as you did, but I knew her. Enough that I see her when I see you. To wonder what she would have been like now. Or if they would still be together. What their kids would have looked like. Yes, it all runs through my head when I see you. But it's not your fault." She took Hazel's hands. "You have never been at fault for not being in that car or for looking like Hanna."

"It would have been better if it had been me. I've not done anything with my life," Hazel said, sounding so sure of what she was saying.

"Tell that to that little kid down the hallway, Hazel. Tell that to Ruston, who doesn't want to live without you. Or the book club, who loves you." Kit took her hands in hers.

Hazel pulled away from her touch. "But they were going to college. They were going to make something of themselves."

"And maybe they would have fallen flat on their faces. We will never know. All we know is that they had what they had and were happy. I have felt guilty about those months before the accident. I knew they were drinking and partying, and I even knew that Jamie and Hanna were having sex. But I have to let go of that guilt because they only had that time. We have the future to look back on the past and regret. They had that day." Kit held Hazel's hands, making sure she heard the words. Then pulled her into a hug, something she should have done so long ago.

"They should have had more time," Hazel whispered.

"But they didn't. We have to be happy with the time they had. Enjoy the memories and forget the guilt." Kit held her close.

"Did she love him? They were having sex, but did she love him?" she asked as Kit finally let her go.

"Yes, I think so." Kit paused and took a deep breath before adding, "She was pregnant, and they were going to keep the baby."

Hazel sucked in a breath. "She never said."

"I think they were going to tell everyone the next week. That's what they told me, but I don't know for sure. They came to me for advice because I'd been there. I should have told you before, but I didn't know how you would take it. I didn't want to upset you." Kit wished for the past, to do it all over again. Not waste so many years scared of the consequences.

"I wish she would have talked to me," Hazel admitted.

"I think she would have, one day. But time ran out." Kit took her hand again.

"Four died that day," Hazel whispered more to herself then to Kit, not pulling away, except Kit was so close she heard.

"What?" she asked in confusion.

"We came into the world as three, and they died as three. I always felt Jamie took my place, stole my place as the third. But maybe he wasn't the third at all."

"Hazel, did you ever think that if you had been in that car, you might have lived? Like Natalie? Survived it? Not everyone in the car died. Maybe you would have been as lucky as Natalie."

Hazel shook her head and said with conviction, "No, I would have died with them."

Kit squeezed her hand. "Natalie felt that she should have died, but she lived. I think you would have lived also. After all, he chose you for Ruston."

"You too?" Hazel gave her a look, and Kit laughed. "Do you think we can get over this?"

Kit let the question hang over her for a moment. "I hope so, Hazel, because I think we accidentally fell for guys who are best friends."

Giving her a hug again, she hoped it wasn't just words. That was the start of them getting over the worst day of their lives. They would no longer just be reminders of what could have been and what had been lost.

CHAPTER 18

SITTING outside Kit's house for hours really seemed like stalking. He was surprised nobody in the neighborhood called the cops. After three hours, he was sure that he wanted her to move to another part of town, one where people called the cops.

By the time four hours had passed, he was pretty sure she was never coming back. That she was staying in Landstad forever.

That was until her SUV turned into the driveway as darkness settled over them. The boys jumped out of the back seat, carrying bags of groceries into the house. Kit was slower as she got out and went to the back and opened the door to get the last two.

Even from here, it looked like the weekend had gotten even worse after they had parted. She looked exhausted and still had an evening with her kids in front of her. And if she sent him away, she would be doing it all alone, again.

"Kit."

She jumped as she reached into the back seat. Her head came out, and she looked at him. "Thomas?"

131

"Can we talk?" he asked, pushing her aside and taking Josiah from the car seat and handing him to her. Then he reached over and grabbed James's seat to carry inside.

"Are you sure you want to? I was kind of a witch to you yesterday." Heading for the house, she hadn't said yes, but she also hadn't said no. In fact, it seemed that she was inviting him.

"I am." He followed her, watching her dress swish as she moved, Josiah on her hip. His blue eyes looked back at him, then the boy smiled, and Thomas hoped he could get his mom to smile at him tonight as well.

"I didn't order you anything, but you can have my burger, and there are always extra fries." She let him into the house and shut the door behind him.

"I'm OK." Setting the seat down, he took the baby out. He was sound asleep and hot from the drive but didn't wake up. Food was the last thing on Thomas's mind. At least until she was his again.

Kit had removed Josiah's coat, and the boy was now in the kitchen, fighting for his share of the meal. Thomas knew it was going to be the story of his life, fighting for everything.

Leaning his head into the dining room, he said, "Guys, help Josiah while I talk to your mom."

A trio of "yes sirs" came from the room, making him smile. Was it because they were so polite or because they didn't even question why he was there? Did they think he could belong there with them?

Kit took the sleeping baby from him and headed up the stairs. Without a word, he followed her—he didn't even think about it; he would follow her anywhere.

At the first bedroom, she set the baby in one of the two cribs, taking a moment to run a hand over his sleeping form before turning to leave him. Once she left the room, he took her hand and led her to her bedroom. He was surprised when she went willingly, way more willingly than he thought that she would.

Once in the room, he shut the door and leaned against it, mostly because if he went too far into her room, he was going to kiss her, which would then lead to them ending up in that bed. As if she knew what he was thinking, she sat on the bed as far from him as possible.

"I'm sorry, Thomas. I acted badly at Ruston and Hazel's house. I let my emotions take over and ..." She sighed. "I'm sorry."

He had thought it would take more than a second to win her over, to get her to forgive him. Instead, she was instantly asking for forgiveness from him. This wasn't even close to how he had thought this conversation would go.

"Kit, it was my fault, all of it. I shouldn't have forced you to spend time with Hazel. I knew you weren't ready. I know how much it affects you, and I completely disregarded that and forced you into a situation you weren't ready for." He didn't leave the door because if he touched her, he would be lost.

Kit shook her head. "He's your friend. I should be able to spend time with him and his wife, no matter who she is."

"Kit, we haven't been dating for a week. Yes, it's great, and I'm completely head over heels for you, but it has been a week. I should have been able to spend four days without seeing you, I know that. Asking you to go to Ruston and Hazel's wasn't right. It wasn't even like I needed to introduce you. You know them both." He ran his fingers through his hair, frustrated because he knew he wasn't making any sense.

Standing up, she took a few steps toward him. "Thomas, you were right in forcing me. Since I left you, I realized I needed to let go of my guilt. I'm really trying to just let it go. I know it won't happen today or even tomorrow, but one day. I talked to Hazel today. We discussed some things that needed to be said. I mean, we're not best friends, but I think we're beginning to put it behind us. Neither of us want to be what comes between you and Ruston."

"Kit, you'll never come between us. We can have a friendship without the women in our lives. Yes, it'll be easier if the women are there, but we can do it if it's what's best for you and Hazel. I want you in my life. You belong in my life."

"I belong in your life?" Kit asked.

Of course, she heard that slip-up.

"Yes, Kit, since the first time I saw you. I fell completely in love with you that day in the teachers' lounge. You were gorgeous." Taking a step toward her, he had to tell her. How could she not know?

"Thomas, I have five kids. Five." Her smile faltered when she added, "And I don't want any more."

Grinning at her, he said, "Thank God—we have five of them already! Do you know how much college is going to run us? Seriously, they graduate one a year for like forever."

"We?" She bit her lip on the question.

"Yeah, I, uhm, guess we. I mean, if you let me. We, that is …" Maybe she wasn't exactly ready for him to be completely in her life.

She smiled. "Thomas, we're willing to take you on, but we are a lot of work, and we are very little reward. We don't get time off, we don't get to date, and we don't get much time away from being 'we.' I don't want you to become part of our 'we' and regret it."

Walking over to her, he cupped her cheeks in his hands. "You guys are worth everything we have to go through. Because I'm pretty damn sure we will be happy as a 'we.'" He kissed her parted lips, loving that she responded instantly.

Before he could take it further, he heard feet running up the stairs, then a baby crying down the hall. The moment was broken.

Kit groaned, and not in ecstasy. Thomas pushed her back until she was sitting on the bed again. Putting his hands on her shoulders, he said, "I'll do it. You've been momming alone for days now. Let me take a stab at dadding for a while. You can"—he stopped and looked around the room—"read something that isn't visible or whatever you want to do by yourself in your bedroom."

"Nap?" she uttered in exhaustion.

"Your half of the 'we' shall nap." He kissed her forehead and went to the door. Stopping, he turned and added, "A nap would be good for you. Get some sleep now—you won't be getting any later."

Leaving the room before she could respond, he went to pick up the still crying baby and head downstairs. If he was going to be a part of her world, he had to climb in and make sure they didn't drown him. He had to show her he was worthy of being a part of her 'we.'

CHAPTER 19

Laying in the dark of the night in that space between sleep and wake, Kit knew that she was in Thomas's arms. They were securely around her, holding her tight, and she felt safe. Safe from everything around her and everything in her mind. For once.

She had crashed once he had had left the room earlier, only taking time to slip out of her clothes and slide into bed. The night before of almost no sleep and the emotional afternoon had been draining. At first, she had thought the noises the boys made would wake her up, but she had heard nothing, felt nothing. Not even Thomas joining her in the bed at some point.

Now she felt him, every bit of him. She nearly purred in contentment at him being there. But that would require effort, and she wasn't doing anything but snuggling closer to him, letting herself be near him.

Her haze instantly cleared at the sound of James crying down the hall, which was what had wakened her in the first place. Five babies meant that she didn't need a monitor to tell her when one of them was awake; she knew. It also meant she was awake, and there was no more sleep until the baby was asleep again.

Slipping out of bed, she made sure she didn't wake Thomas. He needed to work tomorrow, and she didn't want to be the reason he was tired.

Down the hall, she picked up the little boy and snuggled him to her. He was nothing short of clingy in the middle of the night, always had been. Not that she was complaining. Actually, she loved it.

Minutes later, she was settled on the couch with him, a blanket around them both to keep the night chill from intruding on their special time. Feeds during the day were rushed and done almost without them even connecting, but in the middle of the night, alone, she put her entire focus on him.

Without looking at the clock, she knew it was around four in the morning—as long of a night as James had. Ten to four, then he needed to eat. Or, more importantly, demanded to eat.

Her mind went to everything that had happened over the weekend. Had she thought she could let Thomas go and still see him every day? Not after getting to know the real him, the him who wasn't just a flirt. The man.

"Morning, Kit." He had snuck up on her in the mostly dark room, making her jump, but not enough to miss the warmth that spread through her at the husky morning gravel in his voice.

"We didn't wake you, did we? I tried to get to him before he made enough noise to wake you." She watched him walk toward her. He had pulled on his jeans, but not a shirt, and he looked so yummy like that.

"You being gone woke me, so I came to find you." He sat down next to her, close enough to touch James's cheek. "Important meeting, I see."

"One of my favorites," she admitted. Though she hated getting up in the middle of the night, she loved her one-on-one time with her baby. There was never enough time in the actual day for her to just relax with him. But at night, there were no distractions. Just them.

"The boys want a Christmas tree. We had a meeting about it," he said with a smile.

"Look at you, having your own meetings." She loved that the boys were just as taken with him as she was. But then her busy life got in the way, and she remembered why she never went through the trouble of getting a tree. Biting her lips, she admitted, "But we go to my mom's for most of the holiday, so a tree just takes up space, and we don't even enjoy it on the holiday. We're not even here."

It was the same argument she gave them last year. It had worked. And being pregnant and in the middle of a divorce, she hadn't wanted to do anything for the holiday at all. Not that she was still in the same headspace as the year before, but her days were full enough without adding the Christmas hassle to it.

But looking at Thomas, who was new to the entire kids-at-Christmas thing, she had a plan. "If you and the boys want a tree, you can be in charge of it. I won't stand in your way."

"Is this a test?" His eyes brow shot up in question.

"No, no test. Thomas, you're either all in or not," she told him, because she didn't think he really realized how much the boys were always there.

"I'm so in that I'm going to bring you and the boys to Ruston's parents' house for Christmas." He grinned and then stopped. "Or not. We can just spend the day here or with your family. I'm not pushing you to do what you don't want to do."

"First, I want to know why you want to bring me to

Ruston's parent's and not your parents for Christmas?" She questioned.

He leaned back and cleared his throat. "Because I don't exactly like to spend time with my family anymore. My stepdad is very opinionated, and, in his opinion, I'm not the kind of son he wanted. My mom agrees with him."

"Oh, Thomas, I'm so sorry." She wished he had talked about it with her before so that her problems weren't dominating their time together.

"Nothing to be sorry about. Ruston's family takes me in most holidays, though I do make an appearance at mine, for my mom. We don't talk much, but she thinks she wants to see me. Until I'm there."

Kit knew there was more to it than that, but she didn't push.

"So, Ruston's family is your family, and your sister is even a part of it." Now she understood why Thomas would go there for family time.

He nodded. "Yup, and not a girl for me in the bunch, so I just crash."

"I bet that they don't feel you're crashing," she told him, brushing a dark lock of hair from his forehead.

He shrugged. "I don't ask. The less you know, the better it is."

"You were going to crash Christmas with six other people?" she questioned, because one person can crash a party, seven cannot.

Adjusting the baby, who had fallen asleep, she got more comfortable, loving this quiet early morning talk with Thomas. Heck, she loved any talk or time with Thomas.

"Most of them are small, and nobody would notice. You, on the other hand … Rusty has two single brothers still, so I would have to keep my guard up." He touched her chin with his finger.

"I'm pretty sure you have nothing to worry about." She wasn't looking at anyone else when Thomas was around. Hadn't been able to since the day she met him.

"I think I'll worry until the end of time. How did I get you to even look my way? What did I do to deserve you?"

"Don't talk like that, Thomas. I am …" She stopped, not knowing what she was even going to say.

He pulled her into his arms, and she felt safe again as he rearranged the blankets around them. James slept securely in her arms still, his little body warming her suddenly cold body.

Thomas kissed her head as she rested it against his chest. "Tell me about Jeff. You never talk about him."

"What's to say? He died." She hated talking about him.

"Do the boys look like him?" Thomas asked.

"No, none of them. They look so much like me, it's scary." She stopped and breathed, just breathed, then shut her eyes. "Justin has his personality, all of it. Cocky and full of himself, never wrong. Then, with a flip of a switch, he's as sweet as can be. JJ sometimes does something, a hand motion or a stance, and all I can see is Jeff in front of me. How can something be so ingrained that a two-and-a-half-year-old remembers it? Mimics it? Jacob is the most like Jamie—sweet and funny all the time. His goal is always to make you happy and will do anything to make that happen."

Her words faltered, wishing she could tell him thousands of things her boys did that were like their dad, but there were so few. They barely knew him. In fact, she was sure none had a memory of him she hadn't provided them. And she didn't provide many anymore. She wasn't a good parent sometimes.

"Sometimes, I think about what might have been. What would have happened if he had lived? If he had lived, would Jamie have lived because his brother was around? Would he have still died because nobody had any control over it?" She knew there were no answers.

"Would you have had more kids?" As he spoke, he touched James's hand and let it curl around his finger.

She looked at the dark ceiling. "I don't know. I don't even know if we would have stayed married. He was easy to love, but just as easy to hate. Our relationship was changing. I was growing up, but he didn't want to. He wanted to be back in high school with his buddies every day, only getting to do what he wanted all the time. No responsibility."

"He didn't spend time with you and the kids?" Thomas asked.

"He was the dad. He would spend five minutes with them and think he was dad of the year. Being there when I needed help wasn't his priority. He had better things to do." She hated to speak about Jeff like this. The truth was that he wasn't perfect. Far from it.

"So, he left you with three little kids, babies, and did what he wanted." There was anger in his voice, but she didn't look at him to see if it was in his face.

"I never said anything about it, not once. Back then, I was still learning to be me. I wanted to please him more than to rock the boat. I was weak." There it was, the naive version of her who hadn't been mature enough to be married but was.

"You were young and had a lot going on," Thomas replied, but his words didn't absolve her of everything that had happened.

"His parents accused me of trapping him, that I had the boys on purpose. And I think I did. JJ, at least." Though each of her pregnancies were an accident, they were all a happy accident on her part. She had grown up watching her mom be a mom and wanted nothing more than to be like that. But Jeff wasn't as happy about it and wasn't afraid to tell her his feelings.

"Teenagers get pregnant," he said.

"He dumped me, and I got him back because I was pregnant. I was that girl. My dad forced his hand because I couldn't do it myself." It sounded bad and got worse the older she got. Looking back, she would have been fine raising JJ by herself. After all, she had ended up raising all her boys by herself. Back then, she felt she needed a man by her side.

"You were already pregnant when he dumped you, Kit." She could only nod as he continued. "That means you didn't trap him. Him doing the right thing wasn't a trap."

"I shouldn't have pushed. I should have just grown up and raised him alone. One would have been far easier than three." Her heart hurt just thinking about not having any of her boys. They were all special to her. Her life would be different without each and every one of them.

"Can you even see your life without the other two? Four? This guy?" Thomas was still letting the baby hold onto him.

"A week before Jeff died, I miscarried. It wasn't far enough along to be viable. Jeff didn't try to hide that he was happy. He didn't want another baby. I never told my parents or siblings," she said it quietly.

"You kept the pain to yourself? Why?" Thomas pulled her closer to him.

"Mandy. I couldn't tell Mandy that I got pregnant again or that I lost it." She barely dared say it now to this man, even though he would never tell her sister. For years after Jeff had died, she was the only person who even knew.

"From what I know about your sister, she would have been there for you instantly. They all would have been." Thomas stroked her hair as he said it, comforting her.

"Not then, not … A month before, Mandy had a baby, a girl. It was viable, but she died anyway. Stillborn. And before that, she had many miscarriages, and after. Every time I said I was pregnant, I saw her in more and more pain because all she wanted was a baby of her own. I didn't want to take away from the comfort the family was giving her. She needed it more than me."

"And Jeff was nothing but happy, leaving you to grieve alone. Then he died," Thomas surmised.

"I was so mad at him I didn't care. I'm an awful person who didn't care her husband was dead. I was so angry he left me, me and our kids. All he cared about was being in that band. He didn't care what he was missing at home." The tears were falling, and she didn't even realize she had started to cry. But as the tears fell, she knew she couldn't stop them.

"You're not an awful person, Kit. You were in shock. It started when you miscarried and left you numb to Jeff's death. Numb to everything for a long time, I think." Thomas kissed her cheeks, kissed the tears that she couldn't stop.

"I let his brother die. I didn't take care of him enough to keep him alive." She admitted her failure. The biggest failure to her husband, who loved his little brother. A man who would have hated her for letting him die.

"You cared with everything you have. Things happen that are out of our control. You didn't cause Jeff's death, no matter what was going on in your mind. He made his choices, not you." Thomas bringing them back to talking about Jeff surprised her.

"I knew he was drinking," she admitted.

"Did you get the booze for him?" Thomas asked in a whisper.

"No, he always found his own. Always," she stated. She knew about the rumors around town that she provided him alcohol. But Paul at the Landing would be the first to tell you that was a lie. She never stole from him when she worked there, and she hadn't been of age to buy.

"Then you have nothing to feel guilty about. You are human, and he let you down. You have the right to be angry at him for what he said about the life you created. He was wrong to not support you when you needed it the most. He had to know you weren't talking to your family about it, and yet he didn't do anything to help you." His words floated into the nearly dark room, and he let them sink in. He was telling her she wasn't to blame. It was something she had told herself over and over, but it still didn't help.

"But I shouldn't have let that affect me. He died. He might have later. When the boys were older." Even as she said it, she wondered if she was trying to convince him or herself.

"It doesn't matter, Kit. He's gone, and you didn't do anything to make it happen. You just have to live and raise your kids. And you have done that all by yourself. You have done an amazing job at it. He missed that by drinking and driving and by not being there in the first place. That is his loss, not yours." He kissed her cheek.

"I know. But late at night when I'm alone ..." She stopped, unable to tell him her fears.

"I want to be there for you when you're alone late at night. I want you to talk to me. I want to be there for you," he promised her.

"I'm everything you don't want, Thomas," she replied, reminding him that she had more baggage than he would want in a girlfriend. Baggage that he didn't even know he didn't want.

"I never knew what I wanted until I met you. Now I can't understand anything but wanting you and everything you bring with you. All of them. Five boys." He still couldn't believe how many there were, but he was smiling as he said it.

"It's not easy," she admitted.

"You make it look effortless, Kit. And I will have you here with me." He snuggled her closer to him.

"I love you, Thomas. I love that you want to put up with

all this." She nodded at the lone baby in her arms, still sound asleep.

"For you. I will put up with it for you. Forever." He lightly kissed her lips.

Unable to hold in her giggle, she said, "Let's see how you do with the Christmas tree before you commit to anything."

It was only a month away, and she was sure if he made it through this one, he would stay forever. Because Christmas with kids wasn't only a tree, but Santa visits and Christmas programs and nagging kids and too much candy. Not to mention winter break. This month would test any man.

He just smiled. "I already passed that test, Kit. I got you to agree to have one. Now all the kids love me, and so do you. Test passed."

"My kids are harder to please than that," she said, she but knew he had already won them over. It seemed he could charm more than old ladies.

"They fall just as easy as their mom." He kissed her head as the sound of footsteps on the stairs pulled them apart.

As the boys came down rumpled and yawning, Thomas got up from the couch and announced, "Come on, boys, let's make breakfast for your mom before we get ready for school. Does anyone know how to make waffles?"

At the word, the boys perked up and followed him to the kitchen. Watching him go, she couldn't believe that her kids were willingly going into the kitchen with him to do something. With only being asked once. They had truly fallen for him just as easily as she had.

CHAPTER 20

ASHLEY AND KIT were huddled in the corner of the kitchen talking about babies or something. He wasn't close enough to hear them, but they were laughing, and each had a baby in their arms, so what else could they be talking about?

Kit being alone with his sister didn't bother him anymore. There was nothing his sister could tell the love of his life that she didn't already know. Or should already know. His life was an open book.

Over the last month, he had gotten a crash course in parenting that would bring a grown man to his knees. But not Thomas. In the first week after Thanksgiving, not only had Jacob and Justin come down with the flu, but JJ and Kit had gotten it also within twenty-four hours. That left him the only one in the house who could do anything for any of them. And take care of the little two. For three days.

He had successfully kept them all alive and nursed them back to health, just in time for him to come down with it the day he was supposed to meet her parents, which then had to be put off a week. Her parents had been nice enough, but they were a lot harder of a sell than her boys had been. He had a lot to prove to them. So far, he hadn't been successful, but wasn't going to stop trying.

Both women looked over at him and giggled, which made him look at his outfit to make sure he had nothing spilled on it. With two small children, you could never be sure. They were messy little beings, but he already loved them to bits.

"You brought your girlfriend and her six kids to my parents' house for Christmas?" Ruston handed him some eggnog as Thomas checked his fly since the women were still looking at him.

"Five kids." He held up his hand with five fingers and wiggled them. "Her family wasn't getting together today, so we had to go somewhere."

That was a lie. They could have just stayed at her house and let the kids play with their new toys. Far more toys than they needed, but it was his first Christmas with them. He wanted it to be memorable.

In reality, he had wanted to show off his family to the people who had always been there for him. Ruston's family. That Ruston's mom had so willingly accepted them into the fold had warmed his heart. This was his family.

"How about your mom's?" Ruston stated and looked out over the group of kids playing cards in the living room. It was a lot.

"We stopped by, then left when Mom said something about all the kids. So, we came here. Always more welcoming." Thomas shook off the memory of his mom questioning Kit like she had any right to talk to the love of his life about her past, which was anything but sordid.

Kit, for her part, had answered every question respectfully, telling his mom everything and far more than the woman deserved. In all, they had stayed exactly forty minutes before they were back in the car heading across town. At once, he knew they wouldn't be returning anytime soon.

After nearly living with Kit for a month, he had finally realized that his stepdad might not have been the problem in his family. It might have been his mom. She had never been the type of mom Kit was. There had been little affection from her as he had grown up. Nothing Thomas had ever done had pleased the woman, and that wasn't going to change.

All those years, he had blamed his stepfather for doing exactly what his mom was doing. They had treated him the same way, and he knew he deserved better.

And he realized that his step-kids did too. So, Thomas had decided he could change himself. Become the stepdad he had wanted growing up to the five boys he wanted to raise. To be there for every event in their lives, big and small. To be the cheering section they will one day be embarrassed to have.

"Thomas, get more plates for your family," Ruston's dad said in passing.

Thomas smiled. He used to just say get a plate, but now he had to get plates for his family. His family.

It had been barely a month, and he was sure it was just the beginning of the rest of his life. Last night after the kids had opened one present each, he had happily opened a box containing pajamas that matched the boys'. This morning, he stood proudly in front of the tree, everyone in their matching pajamas, though his and Kit's were far less wrinkled than the boys', who actually slept in them. James's was already stained by the time the picture even happened.

"When's the wedding?" Ruston asked with a twinkle in his eyes.

"Which one?" Thomas asked, not paying much attention as he watched Josiah and John Henry playing by the TV. The best of friends, as usual. Every Sunday, they found each other.

"Yours, Thomas. You're in deep," Ruston teased.

"We're giving it a year, then we'll talk," he said, because that was what Kit had told him. He was sure a year was going to be too long, so he would revisit the topic in a few months.

Ruston laughed. "So, you have already talked about it?"

He just shrugged. "We moved into boyfriend and girlfriend status, then we both felt weird about it. It just didn't seem right. Maybe it's because we both work with teenagers. Seems so childish."

Girlfriend just didn't seem like a strong enough word for his relationship with her. Whenever he thought about her as such, he chuckled. She wasn't some teenager he wanted to ask to the prom. She was his everything.

"I could marry you anytime. Oh, and I have the perfect church; she already knows it," Ruston teased him, and he let him. After all, he had teased the man over Hazel far more than he should have.

"Ha ha, she did that twice. We are going to do something else." He knew that already, because they had talked about it one night. Though they didn't have plans for what they wanted to do, there were plans of what they didn't want to do.

"Good luck. I also know her mother." Ruston chuckled.

"I do, too, now. She's a pushover." He had met everyone in her family again formally, except Mandy, who had to work. Her brother had even had a talk with him about treating his sister right. Which made Thomas angry and happy at the same time. That her family loves her so much, except that they thought he could hurt her.

Handing Ruston the cup back, he said, "Now I have to get plates for my family."

Thomas headed off to the dining room to get some of the

good plates. To his delight, Kit soon came in, following him with Ruston's mom. Smiling at them, he asked, "You're not telling Kit about all the trouble I used to get your precious boys into, are you? Because I'm the one that was led astray."

"She was just telling me about how many ladies you've dated. Didn't realize it was in the triple digits," Kit teased him, and he knew she was teasing him because she couldn't keep the grin from her face.

"Did she tell you she has met exactly zero of them? Because I was saving the best for her. You are most certainly the best I have ever found." He kissed her forehead, because he could in no way kiss her lips in front of the older woman. She was more of a mom than his mom was. And he loved that she loved the love of his life more than his actual mom had. Her opinion was far more important than the other one.

"We were not talking about that, Thomas, but I was asking if she had a ring yet. Her hand seems so empty," Joan said with a twinkle in her eye.

"Really, Ruston's mom? You too?" He had always called her that, and she always got a kick out of it. Even if she had five more kids, she would always be Ruston's mom to him.

"Me too?" She raised an eyebrow in question.

Thomas wrapped an arm around his woman and pointed at Ruston. "Your son seems to think I need to have married yesterday, but then again, I have dated my lady way longer than he dated his. But I'm not afraid my lady will kick me to the curb at any moment."

"You're just jealous, Thomas," Hazel said from behind him with a grin.

This was the first time the two had been in the same room since the weekend a month before. So far, the two women hadn't interacted today, and he was sure they wouldn't at all. But the house was full; they could avoid each other easily.

Time would tell how their relationship progressed, but he wasn't pushing it. They had to do this by themselves.

"Of Ruston? Never." Thomas scoffed, and Kit laughed in his arms.

"Thomas is forever jealous of Ruston. It's all he ever talks about. Ruston this and Ruston that. But then again, Ruston got you," Kit said and shifted James on her hip. Thomas took the baby from her. They had gotten so used to switching kids in the last month, he didn't even notice it was happening until he had a baby in his arms, and Ruston's mom was giving him gooey eyes about it.

"I don't think Thomas is looking for a trade, Kit. I thought you would be in Landstad this week." Hazel's eyes didn't miss the hand-off either.

"Nope, Mom and Dad went with Math and Tess to her family in Minnesota, so we celebrated last weekend. We were all there, except my sister Mandy was working." Kit explained. Hazel would already know about Mandy since book club had met recently.

"Is it me, or is Mandy working a lot? Every time we have book club, she's on call. I think it's wearing her down," Hazel said as the two walked toward the living room together. They might not be talking about the past, but they were talking, and that was all that mattered. Maybe they'll one day be able to be friends. What Kit said was lost to the noise all around him, but he happily watched her walk away from him. After all, she had a nice backside.

"A baby looks good on you, Thomas. You and your love going to have more?"

"Five is enough for us. Maybe more than enough, but we'll manage."

"Let the guy get married before pressuring him into kids, Mom," Ruston said.

"Which just means I can pressure you, Ruston." His mom turned on the man.

"Pressure away, but I'm not the one dragging my feet." Ruston answered with a grin, throwing his wife under the bus.

Thomas jumped in to help his friend. "It's been two months; let the woman settle into married life. Be happy with the one kid they have."

"Because you suddenly have five?" the older woman teased him. It was exactly why he loved this woman. She was the best mom a guy could steal from his best friend.

"Hey, what can I say? I'm an over achiever." He shifted the boy on his hip and looked over at his woman, knowing he was going to marry her before the year was out. Her eyes were on him, and he couldn't stop looking at her.

Now he knew he was going to spend the rest of his life being the best stepdad these kids ever had. Heck, he didn't even want to be a stepdad, but a real dad. So what if he'd missed part of their lives. He hoped that when they looked back on growing up, they remembered him always being there for them.

Just like their mom, who he would be spending the rest of their lives proving that she was the center of his world. That everything about her was exactly right for him. Every box checked.

An older woman with a handful of kids. Who could ask for anything more?

EPILOGUE

Kit nearly choked on the pink fruity punch when her aunt asked. Beside her, she heard the distinct sound of Thomas coughing. It was the first time her aunt Dotty was meeting Thomas as her boyfriend, and her aunt seemed to have cut right to the jugular.

Kit's eyes scanned the church basement, looking for an out on this entire conversation, but everyone in her family was busy taking pictures. It was Math and Tess's baby's baptism, and everyone in the family was there. Which meant it was the perfect time for Thomas to meet her extended family, including her mom's little sister. Her nosy little sister.

Thankfully, Thomas had met her entire immediate family a few weeks before when the family had early Christmas. Which left her and Thomas nearly alone for the entire holiday break. Well, alone except for her kids. But like Thomas liked to point out, they slept sometimes.

Finally swallowing the punch that she wished had some alcohol in it, she answered, "We're not having more kids."

Then she glanced nervously at Thomas before restating, "I'm not having more kids, Dotty. Five is more than enough."

"I thought that too once, then came Kipling." Dotty looked over at her teenager, who was staring at her phone in the corner.

Kit knew for a fact that Kipling was not planned. And she was old enough to listen to the conversation the sisters had when Dotty got pregnant again. Her youngest at the time was almost in school, and Mia had been ten. Dotty had been in tears about having another baby. Kipling was number six, and no one truly knew what her aunt had went through that day. All babies are a blessing, but sometimes it takes just a little getting used to. Kit knew that.

"I think it's up to Math and Tess," she said of her brother, more than happy to throw him under the bus today. After all, he was getting nothing but warm wishes. He had enough karma for a little baby vibe. Except based on her brother's grin today, he would be more than willing to have more babies.

"Isn't she a little old?" Dotty whispered, looking around to make sure nobody heard her say that about her nephew's girlfriend.

"Based on the baby she just had, no. And since she comes from a big family, they might have four or five more. How many grandkids do you have now, Dotty?" Kit asked innocently, except it was the only thing to get her to stop asking about her having more kids.

The sisters had an ongoing battle about who has more grandkids. Kit's mom had started it when Math and Kit's older kids were little, and Dotty had none. But now it was getting even, and Dotty's kids were younger. Case in point, Kipling, who was only four years older than Math's oldest daughter, Hailey.

"Once Mia gets married, she plans to have at least four

kids. Right away also." Dotty was lying, and they both knew it. Mia wasn't even dating anyone, and there was no way she was having four kids. Two was her limit—she said it all the time.

"Who is she dating now?" Kit knew the woman had no answer, but it was enough to actually end the conversation.

"Nobody, but doesn't your young man want children of his own?" Dotty brought the conversation right back to her.

"His name is Thomas Harstad," Kit reminded her aunt, who knew exactly who Thomas was. The sisters talked every day, and Dolly wouldn't stop bragging about Kit getting a boyfriend. After all, Mia didn't have one.

Thomas wrapped an arm around her and smiled at her aunt. "When Kit and I get married, I'll have five kids of my own. I will be there and love them as if they were mine until the day I die."

Kit nearly swooned at his words. He knew just how to get to her heart: through her kids. It was exactly how he had treated them since the day he met them. Since then, he had gotten even more involved in their lives, including talking her into letting JJ try out for baseball and not play soccer with the rest of them. Promising that he would do all the extra driving when spring came.

"But they'll be your stepkids," Dotty said as if he didn't know that he hadn't fathered the boys.

"In my family, there are no steps, Dotty. Just kids." Thomas waved at Ruston across the room.

It wasn't his mom and stepdad who he was calling his family; it was Ruston's. Kit had realized that he had little to do with his own parents and treated Ruston's as if they were his own. And Ruston's family was the Brady bunch version of stepfamilies. Picture perfect.

"Looks like the pictures are done." Looking toward where

her brother and his girlfriend had just been, Kit tried again to distract her aunt and seemed to fail.

"Julia has been keeping to herself this weekend. And no Adam." Dotty zeroed-in on Kit's little sister, who was looking through the pictures she just took.

"He was working," Kit lied. She knew Julia was divorced and hadn't gotten the nerve up to tell their mom. As the only sibling who, until this last summer, was still married to her first husband, she was letting her failed marriage bother her more than it should have. All the siblings knew, but nobody was telling Dolly. That was up to Julia.

"Why don't you go see how the pictures turned out?" Thomas brushed a lock of hair behind Kit's ear.

Though they were here together today, he had stayed the weekend with Ruston and Hazel. Since Julia and her girls were there also, it was a full house, and Kit longed to go back home where it was just them together.

"So, Thomas, what are your plans with our Kit?" Dotty turned from innocent to interrogator in an instant.

"I plan to marry her the moment she's ready. Until then, I'll be the man beside her. Love her, cherish her, and treat her like the queen she is."

Kit controlled herself enough not to throw herself into his arms and thank God that he wanted her, kids and crazy life and all. Her.

Instead, she forced herself to talk to her sister, to get away from her aunt. Thomas could hold his own with her.

Julia was still looking into the camera at the pictures or ignoring everyone, which was probably what it really was. It had been how she had spent Thanksgiving and Christmas.

"How are you?" Kit asked quietly, so nobody would here.

Julia finally looked up from her camera. "Fine."

Kit looked at her closely and knew she was lying, but she let it slide. "Where's Mandy?"

"Around. She barely smiled in the pictures. Something's up with her. I thought after the holidays, she would get better. Not this year." Julia finally looked around the basement full of people.

"Where is Mandy?" Mia asked around a ham bun she had stolen from the kitchen.

"Upstairs?" Kit asked, and the three headed as one toward the stairs. "I didn't even get time to talk to her today."

"I did. She seemed good before church. But then she had to sit by Hue." Mia popped the last of her bun in her mouth.

"What does Hue have to do with anything?" Julia asked of Math's best friend forever. The man had been a fixture at their family events for years. Nobody even noticed anymore.

"Nothing," Mia mumbled and looked into the sanctuary.

"She's lying," Julia announced. The two of them had been close since childhood, but even Kit could see that her cousin was lying.

"Would she leave?" Kit asked, because Mandy wasn't anywhere.

"She kept holding her stomach during pictures," Julia explained and looked through the jackets hanging by the door. "Her jacket is gone."

Mia sat heavily onto the bench along the wall and rubbed her face. "Poor Mandy."

"What do you mean, poor Mandy?" Kit demanded, and Julia nodded her head in agreement.

"Nothing. I can't say." Mia bit her lip, lying.

"Book club secrets?" Kit asked.

"Yeah. Book club secrets." Mia's entire demeanor said she knew what was going on, but she wasn't going to confide in Mandy's sisters. Kit wondered if it had anything to do with Hue. Because he was also suddenly gone.

BONUS EPILOGUE

"Do you have everything packed?" Kit demanded from the front step, her coat loosely wrapped around her in the chilly fall air. Her arms were crossed, and she was glaring at him as if he would forget anything. This wasn't his first trip to Landstad, and it wouldn't be his last.

After four years, he knew her moods, and this one was one he had gotten used to. It wouldn't take much to turn it around, at least for a few minutes. November and January were the months that put her on edge the most. He made a point of lifting her mood when the months were upon them.

"I got it all, Kit. You put me in charge of packing, and I'm now a master packer." Rushing her, he picked her up and spun her around in his arms. His reward was a smile and a laugh. "Your husband, the master packer."

"Master of all things," she whispered, so the kids couldn't hear, though the words were anything but suggestive. She blushed when she realized they had been heard.

Carrying her to the car, he set her down near the passenger door. Opening it, he kissed her, pinning her to the side of the car beside the open door. Groans and boos came from the inside the car behind them.

"Your kids are annoying, Mr. Harstad," Kit whispered in his ear.

"They get that from me." He laughed.

Helping her in the car, he rushed around to the driver seat and started the vehicle. A quick look in the back seat had him counting out the five, because once, just once, they had forgotten Jacob and had to drive the half hour back to get him. At least he was still playing a video game and hadn't noticed it happen. But Thomas made sure it didn't happen again.

Just as they hit city limits on their now-familiar trip to Landstad for the weekend, Kit asked, "Did you remember the bag of chips I need to bring on Sunday to Math's?"

Sunday cookouts with her family happened nearly every weekend, and Math couldn't get enough of his new grill this year. Not that Thomas minded. They suddenly had people to watch the kids, and they could sneak off and make out. And if they were really lucky, make it to second base.

"Might have missed those in the packing, but we can get some in town." He knew they would go to that store more than once anyway. The boys were eating machines, every one of them. Which made him wonder why they were bringing the chips in the first place. "And we have to be back early for Justin's football game on Sunday."

"That is why I kept them all in one sport," Kit grumbled, but she couldn't complain too much. Thomas usually took the boys to all their sporting events. He loved being that dad, the overly loud cheerer who knew every kid on every team. The kids were still in public school because, though she taught in a private school, her kids were not going to one.

In the back seat, he noticed James had fallen asleep. Kindergarten was getting to him, and at five, he was just his mom in miniature. And the three oldest were all in high school and becoming young men who he was proud to call his own. He was even thinking that soon they would be in college and gone, and the house was going to be a lot quieter. Except Josiah was the noisiest one of the entire group.

"Toilet paper?" Kit demanded as if she needed it right now.

"Forgotten, dear. I didn't know we needed it, and we can buy it." He tried to calm her but knew today that wasn't going to happen.

"The store doesn't carry the right kind," she grumbled, not in a good mood this afternoon. Maybe her classes were getting to her this fall. He knew she had a group of juniors she was not enjoying and still had another year with them. But he knew it was the season more than her students.

"We will survive." He rubbed her knee, loving that she had changed into a long skirt for the drive, and said to the boys in the back, "No toilet paper this weekend, guys. Your mom wants it all."

A chorus of "fine" came floating up. They knew their mom was in a bad mood just as much as he did. Nobody even questioned the request. Sadly, it might not even be the first time the request had been made. Four years was a long time, and he tended to forget a lot of stuff.

"If you need to use it, use it!" she hollered back to the group, giving him a dirty look because she did the laundry.

What he had learned about a house full of boys was that they were disgusting. Each and every one of them. Him included, sometimes.

Four years, and they still were making this trip every weekend. Though no longer for the same reasons as before. No longer was Brian Kittson even attempting to see his boys on the weekend. He had, in fact, moved across the state the summer Thomas and Kit got married. In a few weeks, all the paperwork would be done, and the two littlest boys would be Harstads. Brian had been more than happy to give up a few of his kids. He had more now.

The three older boys had chosen to stay Smiths. He wasn't pushing them. It was who they were, and since they were half-grown, it was their choice. They were still his kids, and he was glad he didn't have to share them with another man.

So why still drive two hours every weekend? Because of family.

When they were planning a wedding and looking at houses to buy in the city, Kit had admitted that she didn't want to buy something big and expensive. She wanted a house in Landstad. And before they even got married, they had bought one of the old Victorians just off Main Street.

During the week, they lived in a cramped three-bedroom townhouse that she had before they met and, on the weekends, everyone had their own room and a large yard to boot. And they had all summer there. He had even coached summer baseball the last summer, something he would never have done in town.

But Landstad had grown on him, and he knew a lot of the people there. It wasn't just Ruston and Hazel anymore; it was almost everyone. It felt more like home than where he had grown up. He was happy his boys considered it home.

Kit was trying to read as they drove, which seemed to be the only time she got to herself for that. Her head was bent, and her long blonde hair was hanging over her shoulder, reminding him of that night all those years ago of her sitting on the floor in the church basement. She still took his breath away.

"Stop staring at me." She didn't even look up as she spoke.

"Just enjoying the scenery." He reached over and tapped her nose.

"I'm not scenery," she grumbled out in argument.

"You are more beautiful than the scenery." It was the truth, and not just because there was little in way of actual scenery on their way to town.

"You are still a flirt." The corner of her mouth rose in a small smile.

"Only you get to enjoy it now, Kit Harstad."

Slowly she put a bookmark in her book and closed it, turning to him. "I have seen you flirt with other women. Old women, young women, even my own sisters. Not to mention my mom."

He grinned at her. "Just keeping up my skills, so you don't lose interest."

"I don't think I'm losing interest." She licked her lips, slowly and seductively.

"Good, because I have—" His words were stopped by Josiah asking to go to the bathroom. The kids were always getting in the way of him flirting with their mom. That was why he had to remain sharp.

Twenty minutes later, with no accident from Josiah, they pulled into the driveway of their house. Work kept them away, but they liked their jobs, and there was nothing for them in Landstad. But they would keep doing this forever.

The boys were the first to pile out of the SUV, leaving their parents as they rushed into the house. Not a one took anything from the very back. Four were in the house before James managed to get out of the car to follow.

Both turned to the back of the car and breathed a sigh of relief. Kit whispered as if the car hadn't been full of loud boys the entire trip here, "She slept the entire time."

"I told you, Harstads are sleepers." Thomas grinned at her.

"You are a horrible sleeper. Constantly moving and waking up," she accused, but she was smiling the entire time she spoke, her eyes on the car seat behind them.

"I have yet to hear you complain about getting woken up in the middle of the night. I even know for a fact how you like to be woken up in the middle of the night." It was information he used often. Very often.

Kit grinned the same grin she usually gave him when he woke her up. "You haven't been the Harstad waking me lately."

"I will try harder." He kissed her because they were alone, and nobody would comment on how handsy he got with her. Then, when the baby made a noise, he pulled away. "I will take Joslyn in."

He didn't mention that it might be the three-month-old baby who was usually interrupting the waking of his wife. But then he never complained about their little girl. After a long and heated debate on having another baby, she had won, and they had another one. She was a constant winner in their arguments.

The girl looked just like her mom and brothers. Thomas wasn't surprised that she didn't look anything like him. Nordskovs had a look. But he was OK with it because she looked like Kit, and Kit was gorgeous.

He took the sleeping baby into the house before he headed back out to the rest of the things they had brought that were in the back of the SUV.

"Can I take a walk?" As he passed her going to the house, he saw Kit's eyes were on the leafless trees in the yard. She wasn't going to help him anyway.

"Sure. I'll get the boys to take in the groceries and stuff. Maybe even get them to put everything away." He made a joke, but when she didn't laugh, he knew her mind wasn't on the leaves they needed to rake. Her mind was on the past.

"Thanks, I love you." She headed down the sidewalk in the direction of both Hazel and Natalie's houses. He didn't know who she was going to talk to, but one of them. It was early November, and the anniversary of the accident was here. He could tell by her demeanor she was thinking about it.

Though Jeff's death affected her more, Jamie's was the one she was willing to talk about. Her guilt was still there, mixed with the memories of her first husband. Ever since their first Christmas together, she had been seeing a therapist twice a month, and though she wouldn't admit it, it helped. Except when the leaves fell.

"Hey, bring home soap. I think I forgot that also," he called to her, making her laugh. Needing to see her laugh. They both knew that he didn't remember everything for their trip. Well, anything but his family, he always remembered them. Except that once with Jacob.

"Love you too, Kit!" he yelled even louder, not caring that the neighbors heard. They knew already. After all these years, he loved her. And everything that came with her.

* * *

Leaving Thomas alone to take care of the kids and unload the SUV wasn't nice. But she couldn't concentrate, not today. Even during the school day, she had been thinking about another time and another place.

This year, like the three previous ones, she had told her senior class about the perils of drinking and driving. That, yes, people did it all the time, but you never knew when this was the time you didn't walk away. The time you didn't get to see another tomorrow.

Most had been silent during the talk. Others hadn't paid any attention to her. It didn't matter; it made her feel better telling them, warning them, that they were not indestructible. It was all she could do.

Walking through town, she waved at their neighbor, who

was raking leaves. She should stop and talk, but not today. Today she didn't want to talk to anyone.

Once they made their home in Landstad, they hadn't looked back. Her only regret was not being able to raise the kids there. To have them be Tigers. But they liked their school and friends and loved being able to have friends here.

Josiah and John Henry were still the best of friends, and since adding Natalie's adopted son to the mix, they had turned into a menace that everyone in town was aware of. Kit's only saving grace was that Josiah's older brothers made sure that the eight-year-olds didn't get too out of hand. Her boys always had each other's backs.

Before she had made it two blocks, her own SUV passed her with a few honks of the horn. JJ waved from behind the wheel. Since his brothers were with, they were heading out to Math's to spend time with his son, Mason. There were probably going to be more kids there than just the four, but that was for Tess and Math to deal with.

Waving back, she wondered if JJ was going to tell her anytime soon about the girl he was dating. Since she was from Landstad, and word had gotten back to Kit quickly about the romance. It was why she had Thomas talk to the boys, again, about safe sex. It was during those talks she was glad they had a dad to talk to them, because she didn't want to.

Thomas had been great at the sex talk and any other talk there had been. Not once had he balked at the topic. Never had he uttered a word about them not being his kids. In fact, he usually said they were his and got mad when someone called him their stepdad.

Since the day they got married, all five of the boys had called him dad. Her, 'let's wait a year' had turned into let's do it before school started the following spring. But Thomas was already living with them anyway, and nothing was going to change that.

Now with Joslyn, he was getting to be a parent from conception. From morning sickness right through to delivery. Delivery was the only part he didn't want to repeat. But it had been her worst labor to date. Happily, Thomas was the best labor coach she'd had. Well, besides Mandy, who was a professional.

The baby had her daddy wrapped around her finger, and Thomas was enjoying every moment of it. There was nothing his daughter had done wrong yet, and Kit was afraid he was going to spoil her. But he already spoiled the boys, so why not the girl?

Deciding to have one more had been easy. Once James was out of diapers, and Mandy's book club started having babies, her baby fever got bad. Suddenly, she was the only one in town without a baby in her arms.

Thomas was a pushover, especially when she told him getting pregnant might be hard, and they would have to have sex multiple times a day for months. Suddenly, he was all for it. Sadly, it had all been a lie, and she was pregnant within a week. But they still kept "trying" for months.

Another car drove by and honked at her, but she didn't do anything but wave. Her focus was on the cemetery in front of her. Without looking, she crossed the street and walked through the dying grass with its layer of dead leaves that always covered the ground this time of the year.

Her feet took her to the grave she needed to see today. A grave she had stopped by more often in the last few years than the years that proceeded it. Therapy had helped, she had to admit. But what had really made her see she wasn't to blame for either of these men being in the ground was Thomas. He was the best school counselor she had ever met.

And living with him had forced her to talk—Thomas was a talker.

No longer did she think they had died because she had done or said the wrong thing. Both had made decisions she hadn't even known about at the time that sealed their fate, so even if she had known, she couldn't have stopped it.

No matter what she had learned about herself and others around her, today was still the day she let herself be bothered by it all again. For just one day. Ten years ago today, Jamie had died. With him had been the love of his short life and their unborn child. It was something that only Hazel and Kit knew. At least Kit didn't know if Hazel had told Natalie.

Kit crouched down and looked at the names, tracing them both before standing. Wiping a tear from her eyes, she once again wished they weren't here. That they were just someplace and didn't come home anymore. And maybe happy.

At the sound of a laugh, she turned and looked across the graveyard. A tall brunette and short blonde were sitting in the grass. Even from where she was, she knew Natalie and Hazel. And she knew they were at Hanna's and Henry's graves.

Before she had met Thomas, she would have walked away, giving them the space she wanted. Not wanting to intrude where she didn't belong. But now she felt she belonged there just as much as they did. They weren't the only ones who lost someone special that day.

Leaving Jeff and Jamie behind, she shoved her hands into her pockets and walked over to the friends. Yes, they were friends now. Living in the same town helped, but Natalie demanding they be friends had been the real motivation. Kit still didn't understand why, but she didn't need to.

Waving at her, Natalie jumped to her feet as Kit

approached them. Natalie hugged Kit. "We were just talking about high school."

Hazel got slower to her feet and ignored what Natalie was saying. "Did you guys just get to town?"

"Yes, I came here while Thomas unloaded the SUV." She looked around the quiet, cold cemetery. "I just needed to stop by today."

Kit knew they had both taken the day off. They always did. They even almost always spent it together. Kit wasn't always invited and didn't want to be. She mourned in a different way, alone.

"We watched movies all day and then came here. It just felt right." Hazel walked up to her and hugged her, something that Hazel didn't do. But today wasn't a normal day.

Over the last few years, they had become friends, not best friends, but friends. The past didn't intrude on that friendship. Except today, today they were awkward together again. Tomorrow it would be back to normal.

"We have some with Jamie in them, if you want to watch," Natalie told her excitedly.

Kit knew about the videos and had seen a lot of them over the years. Natalie's dad had been obsessed with his camcorder for the entirety of Natalie's life and had recorded every event she had. Which usually included her friends and her entire class. The movies had been a way for her and Hazel to relive the past.

"Natalie and I are done for the day," Hazel said quickly, noticing that Kit wasn't up for movies. "But we're having a small party at the house for the twins, just cake and ice cream. You, Thomas, and the kids should come." She stopped and added, "If you want."

It was an olive branch, but Kit couldn't bring herself to take it. They didn't need or want her there. A reminder.

Giving her friends a brittle smile, she said, "We just got to town and have a ton of stuff to do. Some other time."

"I understand," Hazel said, and Kit knew she did. They each healed in their own way.

Kit looked from Hazel to Natalie and to the grave between them. On it in the middle of her siblings' names was Hazel's with everything there except the date she died. Because she was lucky enough to live, lucky enough not to be buried here.

They were all lucky to be alive. But Kit knew that life was short, and one day, she would be buried there. They all would. Nobody knew when that day was. Until then, they all had to enjoy the life they had and live.

She had to.

Taking a calming breath, she said, "You know what? Cake would be good. How about I text Thomas to meet us at your house?"

Both women smiled, and as a unit, they walked out of the cemetery and across the street to Hazel and Ruston's house. It felt right being there. It felt good. For the first time that day, she felt the pain of the past slipping away.

That day had changed more than the lives it took. It changed everyone's lives that those that had been lost had touched. Hazel and Natalie were still battling the demons of surviving. The high school still had a plaque by the gym with the pictures of three young people whose futures were so bright until they were over in the blink of an eye. A constant warning of what could happen in a moment.

The accident took the innocence of the town away. An innocence it will never get back. But maybe with its innocence gone, the town had grown up. Or had Landstad become better than it had been before? A place you didn't outgrow or want to leave. A place to belong.

The End

Thank you so much for reading Intriguing .

Are you dying to get back to the book club? Up next is Kit's big sister Amanda Nordskov and her sexy next door neighbor/Brother's best friend in <u>Imperfect</u>.

ALSO BY ALIE GARNETT

<u>Indulge</u>
Craving Winter
Enticing Aurora

<u>Landstad, ND</u>
Invisible
Irresistible
Impulsive
Insuppressible
Intriguing
Imperfect
Irreplaceable

<u>The Great Lovely Falls</u>
Falling for the Single Mom
Falling for his Best Friends Sister
Falling for the Boss
Falling for his Step-Sister
Falling for his Fake Wife
Falling into a Second Chance

<u>Hart Series</u>
Seeing her Pain
Her Favor
Max Valentine is Looking at Me!
Keeping her Safe

<u>Stand Alone</u>

Romancing the Doctor